CRITICS APPLAUD *HOME FIRES*, JUDGE KNOTT, AND MARGARET MARON

"Don't let the down[...] [Mar]on's southern mysterie[...] [...] with their coziness. Behind their honeyed accents, the friendly characters in HOME FIRES have plenty of secrets to hide and grudges to settle."
    —Marilyn Stasio, *New York Times Book Review*

"A wholly engaging blend of country comfort and New South sophistication."
    —*Publishers Weekly* (starred review)

"HOME FIRES is a sterling variation on the classic mystery . . . an entertaining yet challenging novel with a mix of engrossing characters whose intriguing personalities are so absorbing they conceal the workings of a perfect plot . . . conveys truths that citizens of anywhere will recognize as universal."
    —*Durham Herald Sun* (NC)

"The characterizations are shrewd and witty enough to make HOME FIRES (in the Deborah Knott series) the best yet."
    —*Kirkus Reviews*

more . . .

"Maron's whodunit plot is challenging, but it's her unconventional characters, colorful family histories, and an unblinking though certainly affectionate view of the contemporary South that distinguish this well-crafted novel."
—*Los Angeles Times*

"A gentle, intelligent return engagement for Deborah Knott . . . a great character, deep, real, funny, and contemporary."
—*San Jose Mercury News*

"A thoughtful . . . deftly plotted tale. . . . Maron is as savvy about southern politics and race relations as she is about barbecue and family ties."
—*Orlando Sentinel*

"An engaging work by an author who just keeps getting better and better."
—*Raleigh News and Observer* (NC)

"Maron's first Deborah Knott mystery won the prestigious Edgar, Agatha, Anthony, and Macavity Awards. HOME FIRES more than lives up to those standards."
—*Southbridge Evening News* (MA)

"The appeal of Maron's mysteries lies in the charm of Deborah's steel-magnolia personality and the fascination of their surroundings."
—*Washington Post Book World*

By *Margaret Maron*

Deborah Knott novels:

Home Fires
Killer Market
Up Jumps the Devil
Shooting at Loons
Southern Discomfort
Bootlegger's Daughter

Sigrid Harald novels:

Fugitive Colors
Past Imperfect
Corpus Christmas
Baby Doll Games
The Right Jack
Bloody Kin
Death in Blue Folders
Death of a Butterfly
One Coffee With

Short story collection:

Shoveling Smoke

MARGARET MARON

HOME FIRES

WARNER BOOKS

A Time Warner Company

WARNER BOOKS EDITION

Copyright © 1998 by Margaret Maron
All rights reserved. No part of this book may be reproduced in any
form or by any electronic or mechanical means, including informa-
tion storage and retrieval systems, without permission in writing
from the publisher, except by a reviewer who may quote brief pas-
sages in a review.

Cover design by Rachel McClain
Cover illustration by Donna Diamond
Hand lettering by Michael Sabanosh

Warner Books, Inc.
1271 Avenue of the Americas
New York, NY 10020

Visit our Web site at
www.twbookmark.com

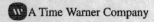A Time Warner Company

Printed in the United States of America

Originally published in hardcover by The Mysterious Press.
First Paperback Printing: April 2000

10 9 8 7 6 5 4 3 2 1

All chapter captions appeared on church signs around the eastern
part of North Carolina and Virginia.

For Andrea Cumbee Maron,
Daughter by law, daughter by love

HOME FIRES

DEBORAH KNOTT'S FAMILY TREE

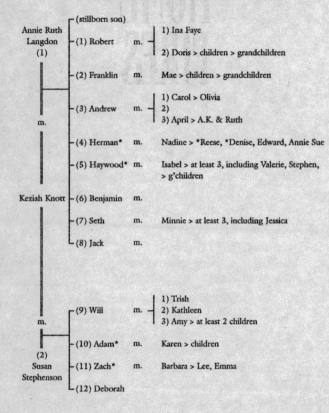

Annie Ruth
Langdon
(1)

m.

Keziah Knott

m.

(2)
Susan
Stephenson

(stillborn son)

(1) Robert   m.
- 1) Ina Faye
- 2) Doris > children > grandchildren

(2) Franklin   m.   Mae > children > grandchildren

(3) Andrew   m.
- 1) Carol > Olivia
- 2)
- 3) April > A.K. & Ruth

(4) Herman*   m.   Nadine > *Reese, *Denise, Edward, Annie Sue

(5) Haywood*   m.   Isabel > at least 3, including Valerie, Stephen, > g'children

(6) Benjamin   m.

(7) Seth   m.   Minnie > at least 3, including Jessica

(8) Jack   m.

(9) Will   m.
- 1) Trish
- 2) Kathleen
- 3) Amy > at least 2 children

(10) Adam*   m.   Karen > children

(11) Zach*   m.   Barbara > Lee, Emma

(12) Deborah

*Twins

❦ 1 ❧

Fire cleanses but the Blood of the Lamb
Washes whiter than snow
— Jones Chapel

Flames are already jetting through one side of the roof. Daddy brakes sharply and pulls his old Chevy pickup right in behind Rudy Peacock. Before he can switch off the truck, I have the door open and am running towards the fire.

The West Colleton volunteer fire truck swings in next to that blazing corner and half a dozen men swarm to unreel the hose connected to its water tank. No water mains or fire hydrants this far out in the country. I doubt if there's even a garden hose. Most buildings this old and this poor, the best you can expect in the way of on-site water is probably a rusty old hand pump out back.

No electric pump and nothing much else electric, judging by the outdated transformer on the light pole and the single thin line that runs down to the small one-room structure where flames leap up against the darkening sky. Where it started, no doubt. Frayed wires. A power surge or maybe a short. The wiring here probably hasn't been inspected since it was installed fifty or sixty years ago.

Typical rural complicity. Long as you pay your bills and no one complains, Carolina Power and Light won't bother you. But get cut off for letting your payments lapse, and they'll make you bring your wiring up to code before turning the power back on.

All this and more rushes subliminally through my mind as I race for the open front door.

Daddy hollers for me to stop, to come back, and I hear one of the firemen call, "Reckon they's still any gas in them old tanks?" Then I'm through the door and into the smoke-filled room.

Someone in protective gear pushes past me with a rough-hewn cross. "Get out!" he yells, but a young, barrel-shaped man gestures urgently from across the smoky room. "The Bible! Grab the Bible!"

I snatch up the big open book and the white lace runner beneath it just as he hoists the wooden pulpit, slings it over his shoulder and heads for the door. Two more men try to move a monstrous upright piano but they can't get the casters to roll and the thing's too heavy for them to pick it up.

Flames lick the exposed rafters only nine or ten feet above our heads and sparks shower down on us, stinging my bare arms. One of the pews in the middle of the room is burning like a solitary bonfire, although the most intense heat radiates from the corner. Smoke chokes me, the skin on my face feels tight and hot, and my eyes are streaming as I look around for something else to save.

Adrenaline pumping, I scoop up a stack of paperback hymn books. Some old-fashioned hand fans are heaped together at the end of one pew and I pile as many as I can on top of the hymnals and the pulpit Bible, then stumble towards the door and out into the humid night air as a burning rafter crashes somewhere behind me.

Daddy breaks free of restraining hands and grabs for some of the fans that are sliding out of my control.

"Don't you never do nothing like that again as long as you live," he says angrily as I cough and cough and try to clear my lungs. His hand is rough as he brushes at my hair where sparks have singed it. "You hear me, girl? I'm talking to you!"

"I'm okay," I gasp between coughs. "Honest."

But then I look back at the burning structure, and like Lot's wife, I am struck dumb and motionless.

More people have arrived and their headlights light up the front of this makeshift church. For the first time I see the swastika and some large dark letters: *KKK* and *NIg-gERS*.

Small g's and the capital I is dotted.

The tin roof gives way with sharp cracks as metal sheets twist in the heat. Flames shoot heavenwards and my silent, involuntary prayer follows them. *"Oh God! Not A.K.?"*

It's the second time in four days that my nephew's had me begging God's mercy.

❧ 2 ❧

When things go wrong,
Don't go with them.
—Faith Freewill Baptist Church

Four days ago, I was in New Bern. In Kidd Chapin's bed.

Kidd's a tall skinny game warden from down east. He's my reminder that there's more to life than courtrooms and campaigns. He's also the main reason I'm finally building my own house out in the country and why I came to wake up that hot Sunday morning to feel him nibbling at my ear.

"I thought you said you bought bagels for breakfast," I murmured sleepily.

"I did. But then I saw this tasty little ear just laying here . . ."

His unshaven cheek brushed mine as he kissed my neck, then moved on to my shoulder and from there to my breasts.

Air-conditioning had us snuggled under a heavy comforter but flames began to kindle along the length of my body and small brushfires erupted wherever his hands and mouth touched. I turned in his arms and stoked the flames that were building in his own body while the fire between us grew and raged and blazed white-hot until we were consumed by wave after fiery wave and came together in a blazing conflagration that left us lying naked on top of the comforter, breathing in cool drafts of frigid air.

His long thin fingers traced the features of my face. "I missed you."

"Me too, you," I said inanely as our lips met again.

It had been way too long. Things keep coming up: his job, my family, his teenage daughter, my political commitments—judges do a lot of after-dinner speeches. A dozen different obstacles had kept us apart since the middle of May, but this late June weekend was ours. I'd driven down to New Bern Friday night and got to his cabin perched above the Neuse River while it was still light enough to see small boats heading upriver after a day of fishing in the Pamlico Sound.

We'd spent most of yesterday in bed, making up for lost time, and though today was Sunday, church was not on our docket.

He pulled the comforter back over us and we lay twined together in post-coital laziness. The whole day stretched before us. Later we would shower, make coffee, have honeydews and toasted bagels on the deck.

But not now.

Now was the afterglow of tenderness and sweet intimacy.

And then the damn phone rang.

Kidd sighed, took his hand from my breast and reached for the receiver.

I lay quietly against his chest, almost certain that it would be Amber, Kidd's fifteen-year-old daughter. She must be slipping, I told myself. Normally, her radar lets her catch us in the middle of making love, not at the end.

From Kidd's casual grumbling, I know that she usually goes five or six days in a row without calling.

Unless I'm in town.

He's always so happy to hear her voice that he doesn't seem to notice how her calls pick up when I'm down and I'm too smart to point out this recurring coincidence.

But this time he wasn't speaking in his indulgent-father tones.

"Just fine," I heard him say with country politeness. "And you? . . . That's good. . . . Yes, she's right here."

He handed me the phone. "Your brother Andrew. Sounds serious."

My heart turned stone cold and a silent prayer went up—*Dear God, no!*

Andrew's nine brothers up from me. He hates any show of emotion and while he did plenty of catting around in his own day, he's like the rest of the boys in wishing I'd quit mine and settle down. Even so, despite his relatively recent respectability, he'd never take it upon himself to confront me head-on about my love life. I could think of only one reason why he'd call me here.

(Please not Daddy. Not yet.)

"What's wrong, Andrew? Is it Daddy?"

"Daddy?" My brother's voice came gruffly over the line. "Naw, Daddy's fine. It's A.K. He's really stepped in it bad this time, Deb'rah."

A.K. is Andrew's oldest child by his third wife. He's seventeen now and will be a senior in high school this fall if Andrew and April can keep him from quitting. Unlike his sister Ruth, A.K.'s not much for the books. Too near like Andrew used to be, from all I've heard.

"What's he done now?" I asked apprehensively. I've been on the bench long enough to see some of the messes a seventeen-year-old can step in and A.K.'s already dirtied his feet a time or two.

"I swear I feel like taking my belt to his backside. He knows better'n this."

His paternal exasperation couldn't mask the worry coming to me through the line.

"What'd he do?" I asked again.

"You know old Ham Crocker?"

I said I did, even though Abraham Crocker must have died around the time I was born.

"Well, A.K. and a couple of his buddies sort of busted up his graveyard Friday night."

"What?"

"They got hold of some beer and I reckon they got drunk enough to think it was funny to knock over the angel—you know the one on Ham's mama's grave?— and then Charles or Raymond, one had a can of spray paint. A.K. swears he didn't do no writing, but he's charged same as the others."

"Charged?"

"Yeah. Bo Poole sent a deputy out to bring him in this morning and me and April don't know what to do. John Claude's gone off to Turkey."

He made it sound as if Turkey was the dark side of the moon and an outlandish place for a Colleton County attorney to visit under any circumstances.

"Did you call Reid?" I asked, since Reid Stephenson is John Claude Lee's younger partner.

"I thought maybe you could come and take care of this," he countered.

Though no kin to the sons of my father's first marriage, John Claude and Reid are both cousins on my mother's side and they're also my former law partners, but the boys have never quite trusted Reid the way they trust John Claude. Maybe it's because John Claude has silver hair while Reid's two years younger than me. Or maybe it's because Reid's personal life is such a shambles and John Claude's stayed respectably married to the same woman for thirty years.

"Call Reid," I said firmly. "He knows us and he'll do just fine."

"But can't you—?"

"No, I can't." I thought I'd made it clear to him when A.K. got caught with marijuana a second time after John Claude had made the first offense go away. "I told you that last year, remember? Judges aren't allowed to represent anyone or give legal advice."

"Not even to your own family? Now that just don't make no sense."

Incredulity was mixed with suspicion and right then's

when I knew my weekend was over. If I waited till tomorrow morning to drive back as I'd originally planned, Andrew and the others would think I cared more about my own pleasure than a brother's need, even though there was absolutely nothing I could do except hold his hand and April's while Reid did all the work.

"His probation's not up yet on that marijuana possession, either, is it?" I asked.

"And he got hisself another speeding ticket last night," Andrew admitted glumly. "I swear I'm gonna lock that boy up myself."

I was ready to hand him a key. A.K.'s not really a bad kid but bad luck and bad judgment aren't helping him these days.

It was going to take all Reid's skills and a kindhearted judge.

"Try not to worry," I told my brother. "I'll be there just as soon as the speed limit lets me."

"I ain't worried," he said doggedly. "It's his mama that's worried. But you'll get him off, right?"

"I'll do everything I can," I hedged, since I clearly wasn't getting through to him about the legal restraints on my help. "I'll call Reid myself and he'll have A.K. out of jail before I get to Kinston, okay?"

"Okay. And, Deb'rah?"

"Yes?"

"I'm really sorry 'bout messing up your weekend."

So was I, but there was no point grousing about it. If you have to do something you don't want to, you're not going to get any Brownie points unless you do it with a willing air. The Lord's not the only one who loveth a cheerful giver and holdeth it against you if you aren't.

My only sour compensation was rousting Reid from *his* bed and hearing a woman's sleepy complaints at being awakened so early. Eventually Reid agreed to go see what Bo Poole, our longtime sheriff, and District Attorney Douglas Woodall had in mind for A.K., but he wasn't happy about it.

"This is not how I was planning to spend my Sunday morning," he grumped.

"Tell me about it," I said heartlessly.

Kidd wasn't happy about it either, but he'd had to cancel out a couple of times himself because of Amber's last-minute demands, so he tried to be a good sport.

He poured me a mug of coffee for the road, stowed my overnight case in the back of my car, and even managed a crooked smile as he watched me fasten my seatbelt, but his voice was wistful.

"You ever wish you were an only child?"

"Frequently," I sighed.

Old Highway 70 between New Bern and Kinston used to be as straight as a piece of uncooked spaghetti and fun to drive even if it was only two lanes and complicated by the small towns of Tuscarora, Cove City and Dover. The new highway is a well-divided four lanes and bypasses the towns, undulating lazily through flat monotonous stands of wax myrtle and marsh grass, then on past Weyerhaeuser pulpwood farms, every tree the same height and as regularly spaced as pickets in a fence.

Traffic was spotty this early in the day. By mid-afternoon it'd be one pickup or minivan after another pulling boats of all sizes and configurations back to Raleigh, Durham or Greensboro. At eight-thirty on a Sunday morning, though, most vehicles were heading east and I had the westbound side of the highway pretty much to myself.

Plenty of time to think about the aggravation of being at the beck and call of eleven older brothers.

Not to mention their wives and children.

Knowing that every time I turned around, the turning was endlessly discussed and dissected.

Nevertheless, I'd lied when I told Kidd I wished I was an only child. I'd had a taste of it my eighteenth summer, the summer Mother was dying, and I didn't like it one little bit.

All the boys were caught up in their own lives then—several of them newly married or lately divorced, babies coming thick and fast, crops to house. That was their excuse anyhow. Mainly it was that they were too inarticulate with grief to talk to me or Mother.

She scared them the way she blazed with urgent purpose that summer. So many things to set in order before she died, from boxes of loose snapshots to closets full of shoe boxes, to secrets that no one wanted to hear except me.

"Go," she said one muggy Sunday afternoon when I was desperate to get out of the house, to go swimming, to be eighteen and hang out with my friends even though they didn't know what to say either. "I'll be all right for a few hours."

But I couldn't bear to leave her alone.

Several of the boys and their wives and children had come for dinner after church, but they all left as soon as the dishes were done, terrified that Mother would make them talk about the cancer that was killing her. Even Daddy had gone off somewhere.

"Don't blame them," she said. "It takes some getting used to. They'll be here when we need them."

And she was right. They were. By the end of the summer, every son and stepson had let her say to him the things she needed to say and they did their best to shore me up when her voice went silent and—

I realized that my eyes were misting over and I fumbled in my pocket for a tissue.

I also realized that the needle on my speedometer was sitting on eighty-five and immediately took my foot off the gas till it settled back to a sedate sixty just as I passed under a cloverleaf. A white Crown Victoria was coming down the on-ramp and I moved over into the left lane so the driver could get in without slowing down.

As he passed me on the right, I glanced over and saw the unmistakable silhouette of a state trooper's hat. A portable blue light sat on the dashboard. He gave me an approving nod for my courtesy. I gave a polite nod back and took a sip of my now-cold coffee.

My cousin Sue's always saying she'd rather have my luck than a license to steal.

Two minutes sooner and that blue light would've been flashing in my rearview mirror.

Doesn't look good for a judge to get a speeding ticket, especially since I sometimes feel as if every tenth driver licensed by the state of North Carolina has probably made an appearance in my courtroom.

Drunk drivers, hopheads, the myopics who cautiously take their half of the road down the middle, and the frustrated zip-arounds in perpetual search of wide-open lanes—they're almost enough to make you want a Sherman tank when you get out on the four-lanes. As it is, I find myself driving a lot more defensively since I took the bench and had my eyes opened to just how much stupidity and road rage are out here sharing the highway with me.

("Yeah?" said Jimmy White when I voiced that observation last week. Jimmy's been servicing my cars ever since I took a curve too fast in front of his garage when I was sixteen. "You passed me last week on Forty-eight like I had my car in Park with my foot on the brake.")

("I didn't say I was driving slower," I said sheepishly. "Just more defensively.")

(He grinned and shook his head at me. "Any more defensive, girl, and you'd've been airborne.")

I consider myself a safe driver, courteous and mindful of others, and I'm trying really hard to keep close to the speed limit; but in all honesty, it's too easy to go with the flow and unless I keep my mind on it or put the car on cruise control, I don't always succeed.

A.K. could use some of my luck, I thought wryly as the unmarked patrol car exited at the next overpass.

Poor A.K.

And poor Andrew, too.

It's hard for him to ask for help. According to Aunt Zell, it's because he didn't get to be a baby very long. Daddy's first wife was a hard worker, but she was also a baby machine, kicking out one son after another at regular intervals like some sort of predictable assembly line. Andrew was the third of her eight boys, and less than two years after he was born, he was displaced not by one baby, but by two—Herman and Haywood, the "big twins," so called because they're older than Adam and Zach, the "little twins" who were born to my mother eleven years later.

"There wasn't any room on Annie Ruth's lap for even a knee baby," says Aunt Zell, and she's always had a soft spot for Andrew, even when he was sassing Mother and talking back to Daddy and ran off and got a Widdington girl pregnant before he was nineteen.

I only met Carol once. Her daddy forced the marriage when he heard she was expecting, but she got a divorce as soon as the baby was born. A little girl.

Olivia.

I've only met her once, too.

Carol took her and ran before the ink was dry on her divorce papers. Can't say I blame her when I hear how wild Andrew was back then, always getting drunk and picking fights. He saw the inside of Colleton County's jailhouse more than once during those years. His second marriage didn't last much longer than the first, but at least there were no children.

April is his third wife, a sixth-grade schoolteacher who's closer to my age than his. She gentled him, brought him back into the family, helped him settle down to farming with Daddy and the boys.

Hell, he's almost a pillar of the community these days. With time, I expect A.K. will be, too.

❖ 3 ❖

The wages of sin never go unpaid.
        —Tabernacle Freewill Baptist Church

At my request, Doug Woodall had hastily calendared A.K.'s case for the following Wednesday afternoon. Since Luther Parker was sitting that session, Reid decided to go ahead with it rather than take his chances on getting someone more hard-nosed.

He'd tried to get A.K.'s trial separated from his buddies, but that hadn't worked. Luther Parker was the candidate who beat me in a runoff primary a couple of years back, when I first ran for district court judge. He not only beat me in June, he went on to beat the white male Republican candidate in November to become the district's first black judge.

I rushed through my own calendar and slipped into the back of Courtroom 2 as the case in front of A.K.'s was winding down.

The defendant here was a black youth who looked to be no more than sixteen or seventeen and he must have been found guilty of the charge because Parker was listening to a plea for leniency from a man who wore black pants and a short-sleeved white shirt with a dark red tie. From his words and measured tones, I immediately knew he was a preacher.

His back was to the spectators and I couldn't see his face until he turned to gesture to an elderly black woman seated several rows behind him. I know most of the preachers in this district, black and white, but this face was unfamiliar. His skin was only a shade or two darker than mine, there was no gray in his hair and he was built like a linebacker. Yet there was a compelling gentleness in his voice when he spoke of the boy's first lapse from the path of righteousness that his grandmother had set out for him.

"What's the charge?" I whispered to the bailiff who'd opened the door for me.

"Shoplifting," he whispered back. "Stole some of them electronic gizmos from the Wal-Mart. Worth about twenty dollars each."

"This *is* his first offense, isn't it, Ms. DeGraffenried?" asked Luther Parker.

"But not his last if the law doesn't come down hard before he starts thinking that coming to court is no more onerous than sitting through one of Reverend Freeman's sermons," Cyl said sweetly.

"Sorry, Sister DeGraffenried," Freeman said with feigned contrition. "I didn't realize you were one of my congregation."

Some of the attorneys and police personnel sitting on the side bench grinned. Reid was sitting there, too, but I was glad to see that he didn't join in the ripple of mirth. He was finally getting some smarts about Assistant District Attorney Cylvia DeGraffenried, who was prosecuting today. I'd have been a lot happier if it was any other member of Doug Woodall's staff, or even Doug himself.

Cyl is all things bright and beautiful. She prepares every detail of her cases, is up on precedents, and has a win/loss percentage that would look good on anybody's scorecard. Mid-twenties. Law degree from Duke. Classic beauty. Drop-dead size-six figure. She even has what my African-American friends tell me is "good" hair. It waves above her large brown eyes and falls softly around her perfectly oval, dark brown face.

That's the only thing soft about her.

No sense of humor and even less compassion.

"Mitigating circumstances, Your Honor," defense pleads.

"Rationalization," she snaps back.

And tough as she is on white offenders, she's even tougher on blacks. Especially young black men.

We still have a couple of white judges who like her attitude. Although less quick to agree when it's a white face, they nod solemnly when she pushes for the maximum sentence for a black one.

The rest of us have quit trying to get DA Douglas Woodall to rein her in.

"Is she unprepared? Shaky on her precedents? Prosecuting on frivolous charges?" he asked me when I first complained that his new ADA ought to ease up.

No, no, and no, I had to admit.

"Number four in her class," he said happily. "Sharp young black woman like her, she could be clerking for one of the Justices up in Washington. Or pulling in high dollars at some politically savvy law firm. I won't be able to keep her once she decides where she wants to go. In the meantime, I'd be a fool if I did anything to rush her."

The last time I grumbled, Doug just smiled and murmured something about approval ratings.

"You know how good she makes him look to the black electorate?" asked the pragmatist who sits on one side of my head.

The preacher who paces up and down on the other side nodded his own head sagely.

That was two years ago and Cyl DeGraffenried's still here. Still pushing for the max even when the offense is minimal. My sister-in-law Minnie's convinced that Cyl's a closet Republican, since most of the courthouse is Democrat and she seldom socializes. Oh, she comes to every official function, but I've never seen her actually enjoying herself or dishing with any of our colleagues.

No, Cyl DeGraffenried's the cat that walks alone, and, like most of my fellow judges, I've almost quit wondering why she hasn't yet moved on to bigger things. As a rule, I just ask her what the State's recommending in the way of punishment and then cut it in half.

Happily, Luther Parker is usually of the same mind even after all these years of practicing law. On the other hand, he's not a fool either.

"You're new to Colleton County, aren't you, Reverend Freeman?"

"Yes, sir. My family and I were called to Balm of Gilead about six weeks ago."

"From Warrenton, I believe I heard somebody say?"

"Yes, sir."

"So it might be it's a little early for you to know this young man as well as you might think you do?"

"Man looketh on the outward appearance, Your Honor. God has shown me his heart and it's a good heart."

Coming from just about anyone else, those words would have sounded sanctimonious as hell, but somehow the Reverend Freeman made them sound earnest and sensible.

Luther Parker nodded and spoke to the boy. "Ten days suspended on condition that you pay costs, make restitution to Wal-Mart, do twenty-four hours of community service and meet with Reverend Freeman here for counseling once a week for the next six weeks." He glanced at the preacher. "If that's agreeable with you, sir?"

"His grandmother and I thank you for your compassion." He put his broad hand on the boy's shoulder. The youth straightened himself and said, "Thank you, Judge."

"Don't let us down, son," said Luther, who really can be a softie at times.

As the charges were being laid out against my nephew and the other two boys, I took a seat on an empty back bench and hoped that some of Luther's grandfatherly compassion would slop over onto A.K. and his two accomplices.

Raymond Bagwell was eighteen, Charles Starling was

twenty, three years older than A.K. Both white. The three of them were charged with a Class I misdemeanor—desecrating gravesites.

"More specifically, Your Honor," said Cyl DeGraffenried, "they knocked over gravestones and used spray paint to deface the walls of a small family cemetery near Cotton Grove."

Several members of the offended Crocker family filled the first two rows of benches behind the prosecutor. Old Mrs. Martha Crocker Rhodes was purple with outrage. As Cyl read out the charges, Miss Martha nodded vehemently and filled in around the edges with low mutters about white-trash ne'er-do-wells who could commit such lowdown, snake-belly acts of vandalism on the graves of her forebears.

The mutters were mostly directed at A.K.'s cohorts since the Crockers were Cotton Grove neighbors and Andrew and Daddy had marched A.K. over there on Sunday afternoon so he could apologize for his part in the vandalism and promise to help put things right.

Now April, Andrew and Ruth, A.K.'s younger sister, sat in the front row behind the defense table, along with my brother Seth and his wife Minnie. Daddy sat straight as an iron poker between his two sons and kept his clear blue eyes fixed on the back of A.K.'s head. We'd tried to keep him from coming, but it was like trying to keep the wind from blowing. "I come for Andrew and I reckon I can come for Andrew's boy, but I sure hope he ain't gonna mess up as many times as Andrew did," he said.

I recognized the Bagwell boy's father and there was a

faded woman about my age who might have been Starling's mother. They had the same rabbity-looking features. Small noses in forward-pointing faces. Slightly buck teeth.

April had good cause to worry about the company A.K. was keeping these days. Both his friends had dropped out of school and both were working dead-end jobs for minimum wages.

When they worked.

I gathered that the Bagwell boy was steadier but that young Starling seemed to get fired a lot or walk off a job in a huff. Why he'd picked on the Crocker graveyard was anyone's guess, but A.K. said it was Starling's idea.

In his day, old Abraham Crocker had fathered a tribe at least as large as Daddy's. Even if A.K. hadn't been a defendant, I probably could have recused myself from hearing this case since my brother Haywood's wife Isabel is Miss Martha's niece and one of Daddy's great-uncles had married a Crocker girl a hundred years ago. On the other hand, any judge whose family's been in Colleton County this long would be just as likely to have some connection to the Crockers either by blood or by marriage, and for all I know, looking at Luther's light brown skin, there could be a Crocker or two perched in his own family tree.

In fact, if we went looking hard enough, he and I both could probably even find a personal connection to the other two defendants as well. A pre-Revolution name doesn't automatically guarantee an unsullied report card—my own family's living proof of that. Bagwell and Starling might be old Colleton County names, but both these boys had stood before me since I came to the bench. Until today though, it had been for minor things: speeding, broken taillights, driving with open beer cans inside the car, barroom brawling, possession of marijuana—the usual et cetera young men keep getting hauled in for till they either settle down with a good woman or cross over the line between hurting themselves and hurting others.

This sort of destruction was pushing that line.

Reid might not have been able to separate the cases, but he was there solely to protect A.K.'s interests. Ed Whitbread was acting for the other two.

"How do your clients plead?" Luther Parker asked them.

"Not guilty," said Ed Whitbread.

"Guilty with mitigating circumstances," said Reid.

The arresting officer had color Polaroid pictures of the damage, a spray can of green paint abandoned at the scene, and a statement from the Home Depot clerk who'd sold five cans of it to Raymond Bagwell the afternoon the incident took place. (The police were unable to find who'd sold them the twelve-pack of Bud whose empty cans lay scattered among the gravestones.)

Cyl laid out the facts for Luther Parker as briskly as if she were prosecuting the Oklahoma bombing.

Overkill.

But she sure made a believer out of the defendants. A.K.'s sandy blond head was buried in his hands. When she rested her case, Luther turned to defense counsel. I could tell that Ed Whitbread was ready to throw in the towel then and there, but Reid was still defending A.K.

against the spray painting. He introduced the shirts the three had been wearing that night. Bagwell's and Starling's shirts both had a fine mist of green paint across the front. A.K.'s didn't.

"He was there, Your Honor," Cyl said. "Who actually did what is irrelevant. He may not have held a paint can, but he acquiesced by his very presence."

Luther agreed, and when defense rested he pronounced all three of them guilty.

Reid made a game plea for mercy.

"They did not go there that night intending any disrespect," he said. "But you know how boys are, Your Honor, when they get out together and you add a little beer. They start egging each other on. Mr. Bagwell bought that paint for a job he was doing, not to deface private property, but one thing always leads to another, doesn't it? These boys are sincerely sorry for what they did. My client has personally apologized to the Crocker family and he intends to do everything he can to restore their burying ground to its original state. His grandfather's already hired a stone mason to see if the angel can be repaired and the cost will come out of my client's pocket."

"If they didn't intend any mischief," said Cyl, "why did they go armed with spray paint? And as for what happens when boys 'add in a little beer,' that's precisely why the state of North Carolina prohibits the sale of alcohol to anyone under the age of twenty-one. They were breaking the law the minute they popped the top on the first can."

Luther Parker looked from one boy to the other, then back to Cyl. "Previous convictions, Ms. DeGraffenried?"

"Level Two, Your Honor. Mr. Knott has had one previous conviction, Mr. Bagwell's had three and this will make Mr. Starling's fifth."

She handed up their records. All were misdemeanors. I'd looked it up. And A.K. had finally had a bit of luck. His suspension on the marijuana charge had been up at the end of May so that wasn't going to land on him.

"And what's the State asking?"

"All three have had at least one suspended sentence, they've had fines, they've had community service, and they're still breaking laws, Your Honor. The State feels maybe it's going to take some jail time before they get the message. We're asking the full forty-five days."

In other words, the maximum sentence for a Level 2, Class I conviction.

Before Luther could rule, a soft, apologetic voice interrupted from one of the rear benches. "Your Honor, may I speak?"

"Mrs. Avery?"

Till that moment, I hadn't noticed the small-boned white woman seated across the aisle from me at the back of the courtroom.

Luther motioned for her to come forward and, as always, Grace King Avery reminded me of the self-effacing little guinea hens that used to run around my Aunt Ida's farmyard. She has the same tiny bones and the same dainty steps as one of those guineas picking its way across the grass. Instead of smoothly rounded gray feathers, she still wore her gray hair in a slightly bouffant French twist I remembered from twenty years ago, and her neat powder-blue shirtwaist could have been the same one she was wearing the first day I stepped into her sophomore English class.

She was never my favorite teacher. Passive-aggressive people have always irritated the hell out of me. After ten minutes I'm ready to run screaming in the opposite direction. Besides, what teenager wants to concentrate on gerunds and punctuation or split infinitives and diagrammed sentences when pheromones are swirling through the classrooms and your parents have finally agreed that you can get in a car with a boy if there's another couple along and you're still agonizing over who that boy should be?

But a single-minded and determined nagger was evidently what it took to give us a mastery of the mechanics of English by year's end, something none of our more straightforward or sweet-tempered teachers had managed up till then.

Law briefs are a lot easier to read and write when you have a sound grasp of semicolons and understand the difference between subordinate and independent clauses. I have blessed Grace King Avery more than once over the years. (And it's always Grace *King* Avery, as if she thought the Kings really were royalty instead of merely hardworking farmers who'd acquired a hundred acres of sandy farmland last century and managed to hang onto it throughout this one.)

"Your Honor, before you pass judgment on these

young men, could I say a word on behalf of Raymond Bagwell?"

"Certainly, Mrs. Avery," Luther Parker said. "Was he one of your students?"

"He was." Her neat head bobbed in Bagwell's direction and her bright eyes softened with indulgence. "And while he may not have applied himself and finished school, he's smart with his hands and he's not a bad boy. His grandfather farmed with my Grandfather King and so did his father. All good, hardworking, Christian people."

She gestured to the weather-beaten man sitting behind my family. He gave a short nod as if embarrassed, and I almost expected to see him pull his forelock.

"And now that I've moved back to the King homeplace, Raymond's helping me fix up my house and my yard. Mr. Stephenson is right when he says Raymond didn't buy that paint to do bad. I gave him the money to get it for some lawn chairs he's painting for me. He always arrives on time and he gives me a full hour's work for a full hour's pay. It's just that on the weekends . . . well, he maybe drinks too much and he does tend to keep bad company, but if you could find it in your heart to give him another chance?"

It was that same wheedling tone of old. (*"Now, Deborah, if you could just diagram the rest of those sentences/rewrite this paper/correct all the punctuation/pay attention to your pronoun cases . . . "*) If the Bagwell boy worked for her full-time, I knew he was earning every penny. That can of misused spray paint would come out of his wages, too.

In all fairness though, the King homeplace has really begun to gleam since she retired from teaching this past May and moved back there. Her penny-pinching bachelor brother hadn't spent a dime on it since their mother died fifteen or more years ago and people say he left Mrs. Avery quite a nest egg. From what I'd heard of the way she's been spending this last month, that nest egg must have been laid by the golden goose.

Her husband left her nicely fixed, too, and the house they'd shared in Cotton Grove was bigger than this one even though they had only the one daughter, now married and living in D.C. But that house had been built in the fifties—"No history," Mrs. Avery used to say with a sniff. (She was big on history, especially family history, and had done her genealogy back to England and the sixteenth century.) As soon as her brother was decently buried in the cemetery behind Sweetwater Baptist, she'd put the house in Cotton Grove up for sale and moved back to her childhood home like a hereditary princess reclaiming her birthright.

Every time I drive out to check on the progress of my own house, I see something new on the King homeplace. New roof for the house, new tin for the barn, new screening for the back porch, fresh paint everywhere, not just on those old wooden lawn chairs everybody used to own. It's going to be a color spread out of *Southern Living* by the time she's finished.

Luther thanked her for coming to speak on the young man's account, then had the three stand.

From behind, A.K. was the most solidly built. The

Starling boy was a little taller and bone skinny, with long yellow hair tied back in a ponytail. Young Bagwell, with his closely clipped brown hair, was shortest, but beneath his dark blue T-shirt there was a wiry strength in his shoulders as he and the others listened to Luther's short lecture on the sanctity of private property and the respect due to the dead.

"The District Attorney thinks it's going to take some time in jail for you to get the message and I'm afraid I agree with her this time," he told them.

Based on the number of each boy's previous convictions, A.K. was going to be spending the next three weekends in jail. The Bagwell boy would do four weekends and Charles Starling got five. That meant they would report to the jail at six P.M. on Friday evenings and get out at five P.M. on Sunday.

I'd warned Andrew that this was what would probably happen, although Luther had actually gone a little easier than I'd expected.

Andrew nodded grimly as he heard the sentence pronounced and I foresaw a rough July for A.K. Andrew would keep him humping in the fields all week, then jail for the weekends.

Luther also sentenced them each to twenty-four hours of community service, "and that's not counting the time it takes for you three to clean up the Crocker family's cemetery. You can thank Mrs. Avery that I'm not giving you the full forty-five days of active time."

Starling looked indifferent, but Bagwell and A.K. shot Mrs. Avery shamefaced smiles.

Luther adjourned court and as I started to join my family, who had headed out the rear door, Mrs. Avery stopped me.

"I wasn't speaking up for that trashy Starling boy, Deborah—he always *was* a problem—and I never taught your nephew. I only meant Raymond."

"I understand, Mrs. Avery, but they were equally guilty. Judge Parker couldn't punish one much more severely than the others."

"I don't see why not," she said, her small head shaking from side to side in disapproval. "I really don't see why not when Raymond's such a nice boy, and that Charles Starling's a wicked influence."

"Nevertheless—"

"The day he quit school, he broke the antenna on my car and put a big long scratch right across the trunk. I *know* it was he even though Sheriff Poole couldn't prove it. And all because he flunked my English class and couldn't stay on the baseball team. As if it were *my* fault he wouldn't do his work. And now here's more willful vandalism. They really ought to send him to prison for a whole year. Give Raymond a chance to be with better boys." She pursed her lips. "And I have to say I'm surprised and disappointed in your nephew."

"Me, too," I admitted. "Maybe this will be a wake-up call for all of them."

"You mark my words, Deborah. This little slap on the wrist Charles Starling got will be like water off a duck's back. He's going to cause a lot more trouble for those boys before he's finished. You wait and see."

* * *

Out in the rear hallway, Charles Starling had lit up a cigarette. "They all stick together, don't they?"

A hank of yellow hair fell across his rabbity face and short angry streams of smoke jetted from his nostrils.

"How come that nigger gets a suspended sentence and I get five weekends of jail time?" he snarled at Ed Whitbread.

"Hey man, chill," said A.K.

Andrew put a heavy hand on his son's shoulder. "Let's go," he said sharply.

Thankfully, Daddy didn't seem to have heard it.

I sometimes think back to that afternoon and wonder if it would have made any difference if I'd listened harder, taken more seriously all I saw and heard.

"Probably not," the pragmatist says comfortingly.

"You can't know that," says the stern preacher. "Arthur Hunt might still be alive if you'd paid more attention."

❧ 4 ❧

Church is a hospital for sinners,
Not a museum for saints.
—Bear Creek United Christian

Out at the farm that evening I asked Maidie, "How come you don't make Daddy buy a dishwasher?"

She gave the glass she was drying a critical squint and then slid it back into the hot soapy water for me to re-wash.

"I don't need no dishwasher," she said. "Not for the few little dishes Mr. Kezzie messes up."

"Oh, come on, Maidie. Daddy's not the only person you cook for, and you know it. Some of the boys or their kids are over here almost every day."

"For dinner maybe," she agreed, referring to the mid-day meal. "But not for supper. You and Mr. Reid, y'all the first in nearly a month and most times if it's some of the family, the womenfolks shoo me out and clean up the kitchen theirselves."

"They better," I said.

Not that Maidie's any Aunt Jemima who'd let them

take advantage of her. She knows perfectly well how hard it'd be to find somebody to fill her shoes should she decide to leave, which, God willing, won't happen anytime soon.

She came to the farm more than thirty years ago, a shy and lanky teenager Mother had hired to help out temporarily while the woman I called Aunt Essie was up in Philadelphia helping her first grandchild get born. Aunt Essie found a widowed policeman up there and Maidie found Cletus Holt right here and both women settled where they landed. Aunt Essie was a generation older than Mother and died a few years after she did, but Maidie's only got about fifteen years on me. She got over being shy about the third day and time has amply padded her once-lanky frame till she's an imposing figure, but she won't sit if there's work to be done and her hands are never empty and idle.

I rinsed the glass and stood it in the drain rack and this time it passed her inspection.

Daddy'd asked me to drive him home from court and once Reid heard that Maidie was making stuffed peppers, he'd wangled an invitation to come for early supper, too.

It was a summer supper right out of the garden that Daddy tends with Maidie's husband Cletus: sweet bell peppers stuffed with a moist hamburger and sausage mixture, tender new butter beans sprinkled with diced onions, fried okra, meaty tomatoes that really had ripened on the vines, and thin wedges of crispy hot cornbread.

Reid ate as if it was the first home-cooked meal he'd had since he and Dotty got divorced. (Since he can't cook and most of his girlfriends don't, he's become shameless about scrounging meals.) He was appreciative enough to answer Daddy's every question about A.K.'s situation, but his appreciation didn't extend to helping with the dishes. Shortly after we rose from the table and Daddy went out to the porch for a cigarette, he took off.

Except for the principle of it, I didn't really mind. Washing dishes with Maidie is always a comfortable task, one conducive to gossip and confidences about all the big and small things going on around the farm. It's one of the ways I keep up with the changing community. As a child, I used to stand on a little stool with Mother's apron tied around my neck to help them wash dishes, scrape carrots or make biscuits. In those years, I had no trouble bouncing back and forth between the rough and tumble of my big brothers outdoors and the soft voices of women working together in a kitchen.

Maidie's also one of my windows on the black community, just as my family is one of hers to the white community.

Desegregation's been a real mixed bag down here. Took away some of the old sore spots, brought in a bunch of new ones. No more separate drinking fountains as when my brothers were little. No more separate entrances to movie theaters or separate seating at bus and train stations, no more "No Coloreds" signs on restaurant doors. We go to school together, we swim at the same public pools and beaches, we work side by side on assembly lines or in offices now as frequently as we have always worked side by side in the fields.

For the most part, the law is followed pretty strictly these days.

The letter of the law, anyhow.

But the spirit of the law? In the back rooms? Under the table or in one's cups? At private pools and clubs? Forget it. There's still plenty to keep us apart, plenty of cautious mistrust and wary stiffness on both sides.

"We may got to treat 'em all equal," says my own brother Haywood, who would never dream of sassing Maidie or doing down any of the black tenants who farm with him, "but that don't mean we got to like 'em all equal."

My brother Ben is convinced that his tenants quit working the minute he turns his back, yet he can come dragging in from the fields, all tired and sweaty, and declare that he's been "working like a nigger," without seeing the irony of his words. Till the day they die, he and Robert and Haywood will always notice a stranger's skin color first.

God knows life would be a lot simpler if we could all wake up one morning color-blind, but we're nowhere close to it on either side. Not by a long shot. We continue to lead separate, parallel personal lives, seldom connecting without self-consciousness, at genuine ease only at points of old familiarity such as Maidie and me here in my mother's kitchen.

"You and Miss Zell still coming to the fellowship meeting Sunday, ain't you?" she asked as she hung coffee mugs from hooks in a nearby cupboard.

"I never miss a chance to press the flesh or eat your

chicken pastry," I said. "And while I'm thinking of it, remind me again where Balm of Gilead Church is?"

She hesitated, then finished hanging the last mug and closed the cupboard door. "Why you asking 'bout that place? You gonna politick there, too?"

"It's not the one next to Mrs. Avery, is it? Oh, wait, of course not. That's Burning Heart of God. And besides, their preacher's that mean old woman, isn't she? Sister Wilson?"

"Sister Williams. Miz Byantha Renfrow Williams and you don't need to be bad-mouthing her just because she's so Holiness."

"Why not?" I argued. "She bad-mouths everybody else and their religion. But Balm of Gilead. How come I can't remember it?"

"Maybe 'cause they used to call it just plain Gilead," she said. "Remember Starling's Crossroads? Used to be a gas station when I was real little?"

That connected. Starling's Crossroads is one of those insignificant backcountry crossings that got dead-ended when I-40 went through a few years back. It'd been dead before that though. That wood-framed store with its two lone gas pumps sat empty for several years until one of the black churches in Makely split wide open over something or other, and part of the congregation came up here and turned the little store into a chapel.

"Starling's Crossroads?" I handed Maidie another glass. "As in Charles Starling, the boy that was with A.K. when they messed up the Crocker graveyard?"

"He might be some of that same bunch. But they ain't

owned nothing over there in fifteen, twenty years. How come you're asking about Balm of Gilead?"

"No real reason," I said. "Their new preacher was in court today to speak up for a member's grandson. I believe his name was Freeman? Seems real sharp."

Maidie made a humphing sound.

"What?" I asked. When Maidie humphs, there's usually a reason.

"Preacher Ralph Freeman's a sheep-stealer."

"Now who's bad-mouthing?"

"You asked me, didn't you?"

I was curious. "Whose flock?"

"Whoever's he can get."

"Surely not any of Mount Olive's?"

Just as I'd been born into Sweetwater Missionary Baptist a few miles south, Maidie'd been born into Mount Olive A.M.E. Zion a few miles north of us and she was fiercely loyal to it.

"They's been one or two drifted over," she admitted. "Ever since they started arguing over getting us on the historical register."

"That still going on?"

Maidie sighed and nodded.

Sweetwater began as a modest turn-of-the-century wooden structure that's been remodeled, enlarged and bricked over so many times that few people know (or care) about its earliest lines, but Mount Olive is an exquisite antebellum building that's been lovingly tended in its original state.

Outside, it's a two-story, white clapboard box with a

simple pitched roof of green wooden shingles. No stained glass here. The tall, one-over-one double-hung windows are rectangles of frosted glass with a beveled cross etched in the center. The only outside ornamentation is a course of hand-cut dentil molding up under the eaves and a large front door that is flanked by plain Doric pilasters and topped by a triangular pediment with more dentil molding. The overall effect is, and I quote, "a harmonious blending of naive Georgian with intimations of Greek Revival."

That's not me talking. That's an article the *Ledger* reprinted a few years back when Mount Olive celebrated its hundred and fiftieth anniversary. The county commissioners had hired someone from State University to do an architectural survey of the county during the Bicentennial back in 1975 and he'd gone nuts over Mount Olive. I remembered hearing Maidie tell Mother how he wanted to have it added to the National Register then and there, but conservatives in the church voted it down.

Martin Luther King once observed that the most segregated hour in Christian America is eleven o'clock on Sunday morning, but it wasn't always that way. Not when Mount Olive was built.

Blacks and whites worshipped the Lord together then. Okay, okay, if you want to get technical about it, the whites did sit downstairs and the blacks did sit up in the slave gallery that ran around three sides of the upper level. But they were all under one roof and they all sang with one voice.

No one quite remembers why things happened that

way, but during Reconstruction, instead of barring its doors to their dark-skinned brothers and sisters in Christ, the whites abandoned Mount Olive and ownership passed by default to the former slaves and the few free-born people of color.

Back then the congregation barely numbered fifteen families. Fortunately for the building, those families contained carpenters, painters, roofers and masons who scrounged materials from their jobs, salvaged what was being thrown away, and used their God-given talents to keep the fabric of the church sound.

By the late seventies, the congregation had grown until even the most conservative members couldn't deny the need for more space. Most churches would move walls at that point, sprout Sunday School wings or do a complete renovation.

Not Mount Olive.

After a fierce debate that brought the church to the edge of splitting for good, they reached a grudging compromise. Since the most ardent advocates for maintaining the church's architectural integrity also had the deepest pockets, that faction prevailed. Not a single new nail got driven into the exterior boards. Instead, they raised money for Sunday School classrooms, restrooms, and a large fellowship hall and the new building went up immediately behind the old. It mimicked the Georgian/Greek Revival lines of the old but inside everything was modern and up to date and the green shingles were asphalt.

This sufficed until Colleton's cheap land, low taxes

and exceedingly elastic zoning regulations, coupled with our easy access to the Research Triangle, made us ripe for housing developments. Church membership is up all over the county, but Mount Olive, perceived as the most middle-class and influential of all the black churches, has really boomed. It now takes two Sunday morning preaching services to accommodate the whole congregation and Maidie says there are many who want to double the size of the sanctuary so that everybody can be seated for one service.

Like our school boards, county commissioners and town councils, Mount Olive has learned that this new wave of people isn't content to sit in the back pews and keep its mouth shut. Unfamiliar viewpoints rasp up against old traditions.

"Been hot words on both sides," Maidie said sorrowfully. "Some folks say the church should be about people, not walls. We a church, not a museum. Some of the new brothers and sisters, 'specially those from up the road a piece, say it's shameful to keep the old slave gallery, say it should have been ripped out a hundred years ago. They don't want to hear 'Go Down, Moses.' They want it all stomping and shouting."

"What about you, Maidie?" I asked.

She shook her head. "I don't know. We getting too big, that's for certain. But I surely do hate to see deacon against deacon till folks start looking for some place more peaceful on Sunday mornings."

I stuck the last of the knives and forks in the drain basket and rinsed out the last of the saucepans.

"So maybe Preacher Freeman's not stealing sheep," I said. "Maybe he's just looking out for the strays."

"Humph!" said Maidie. "They gonna need a whole new flock if they build 'em a real church. That's how come they brought in this new preacher. He raised a new church over in Warrenton and Balm of Gilead's called him to guide 'em to a new building here."

She spoke as if a little makeshift church could suddenly raise enough money for a real edifice. It was going to take a lot of barbecued chicken plates to do that.

She handed me some paper towels. I wiped out the black iron skillet in which she had cooked the cornbread and hung it on a nail in the pantry.

That skillet's been handed down from Mother and Aunt Zell's grandmother and is never used for anything except cornbread, which is why it's never washed. Maidie keeps to the old ways with Mother's ironware. About every four or five years, she sticks the flat skillet and a favorite fry pan on a bed of red-hot coals in the woodstove and burns off all the charred and blackened incrustation that's accumulated on the outside and then she grumbles for a week till she gets them properly seasoned again so that nothing sticks when she's cooking.

Mother was a hard worker—"She had to be, with such a houseful of young'uns," says Maidie—but she had no intention of killing herself to save a penny the way Daddy's first wife had. She cooked and cleaned and washed and ironed and she would freeze and can any fruits and vegetables Daddy or the boys brought up to the house, but she never worked in the fields and she was never without household help. Not just us children, who had chores and responsibilities as a matter of course, but women she hired right out from under Daddy's nose.

Aunt Essie had been his best looper when tobacco was still strung on sticks and cured in oil-fired barns. She could take from four handers, hour after hour, when most loopers couldn't keep up with three. And she did it for sixty cents an hour, same as what the men got for priming the sticky green leaves out in the hot sun.

They say that the morning Mother offered Aunt Essie five dollars a day to come work with her in the house, Aunt Essie handed her string over to Daddy's sister Ida, threw away her tar-gummy plastic apron, scoured her fingertips raw with a brush to get all the tar out from under her nails and said, "God willing, I've done and touched my last leaf of tobacco."

They say Daddy came storming up to the house and tried to lure her back to the barn for seventy cents—a full ten cents an hour more than the men—and she and Mother just laughed at him.

After that, he tried not to brag on who worked hard " 'cause just as sure as I do, Sue'll hire 'em away from me."

" 'Cept for getting you to quit moonshining, it was the best day's work *I* ever did," Mother would say, sharing a quiet glance of mischief with Aunt Essie.

We hung our dishcloths up to dry. Maidie patted my cheek and told me not to be a stranger, then gathered up a second panful of stuffed peppers which she'd cooked for her and Cletus's supper and went off down the path to their house.

It was only seven-thirty, still plenty of daylight as I walked back through the house, down the wide central hall that separates dining room on the left from back parlor on the right where Mother's piano sits tuned and ready. She could flat tear up a keyboard. Although I pick a passable guitar, I never learned to play the piano with more than one finger. Happily, a couple of my nieces are good enough to keep up with Daddy's fiddle and our guitars when the family gets together to play.

My old bedroom upstairs hasn't changed from when I last lived here. Maidie keeps fresh sheets in the bottom dresser drawer in case I decide to spend the night at the last minute, and I'd changed into a spare pair of jeans before supper. Now I picked up the dress and high-heeled sandals I'd worn in court earlier today, slung my purse over my shoulder and went downstairs.

Daddy was sitting on the porch swing. Blue and Ladybelle lay sprawled nearby. The two hounds are seldom far from his side when he's outdoors.

"Ain't leaving now, are you, shug?" he asked.

My Firebird was parked at the foot of the steps, so I put my clothes on the backseat, then went and sat down beside him on the swing.

"I'm in no hurry. Just thought I'd run past and see how my house is coming before it gets too dark to see."

Daddy wasn't all that happy that I was building a house of my own even though he hadn't blinked an eye when I asked him to deed me five acres out by the long pond where I could have a little privacy. He'd never ask, but I knew he wished I'd come back home, move into my old room upstairs, let him look after me as if I were still his precious baby girl.

Never gonna happen.

I haven't lived at home since I stormed out after Mother died. I took a circuitous route through law school and eventually came back to Colleton County, but not to my father's house. Instead I moved in with Mother's sister Ozella. She and Uncle Ash have that big house and no children and we don't rasp each other's nerve endings.

Daddy and I get along just fine these days and I figure it'll stay that way as long as we don't try to live under the same roof.

"Annie Sue said she was going to start pulling wire this week," I said. "Want to come along and check it out?"

He resettled his summer straw planter's hat lower on his silver head. "Well, I was thinking maybe you and me could ride over to the Crocker burying ground first? I'm supposed to get up with Rudy Peacock. See if he can put a wing back on that angel."

❧ 5 ❧

A Bible that's falling apart
Often belongs to one who isn't.
—Westwood United Methodist

Summer or winter, riding with Daddy was always an adventure when I was growing up. I never knew if I was going to wind up in a heated discussion about politics under the shade of a chinaberry tree in somebody's dusty backyard or if I'd be shivering in front of an improvised oil-drum fireplace while my brother Will auctioned off the household effects of someone recently deceased.

The boys love to tell how at least once every summer, usually just before barning time, Daddy'd load them all up in the back of the truck with old quilts and towels to soften the steel truck bed and a large ice chest full of soft drinks and fried chicken and they'd go spend the whole day down at White Lake. "We'd be on the road by first light and not get home till almost midnight, sunburned and wore plumb out."

There are snapshots of the boys clowning on the clean white sand that forms the bottom and gives the crystal-clear lake its name, but none of me in my little pink-and-white-striped bathing suit.

"That's 'cause we quit going before you were old enough to come," says Seth. "Robert was already married to Ina Faye and Frank already joined the Navy."

"So why'd y'all quit?"

Seth's five brothers up from me and the one most tolerant of my questions of how things were back then, but he shrugs at this question. "Integration, I reckon."

"But we always swam together in the creek," I protest.

"With colored kids we knew," he says doggedly. "Kids from around here."

"Colored kids who knew their place?" I ask from my smug perch on the sunny side of *Brown vs. Board of Education.* "What was wrong with those strangers? They too uppity?"

Seth shakes his head. "Actually, it was Ben and Jack didn't know *their* place. They'd never seen whites dating blacks before and they weren't bashful with their words when they walked up behind some at the hotdog stand. Ever notice that little scar under Jack's chin? He got a cut before Daddy could break up the fight. He gave 'em both a licking when we got home and that was the last time he carried us anyplace but the beach to go swimming."

Even though Daddy was a New Deal Democrat who admired Mrs. Roosevelt's "spunk" I've never been totally sure of his rock-bottom feelings on race, but I was willing to bet that Ben and Jack were punished not so much because they'd made a racist slur but because they'd picked a fight over something that was none of their business.

If he has a credo that he's tried to pass on to us, it's Live And Let Live And Don't Go Sticking Your Nose In Stuff That Ain't None Of Your Business.

Some of us still keep getting our noses thumped.

Like his house, Daddy's old pickup doesn't have air-conditioning. I rested my arm on the open window and the warm June air ballooned the sleeve of my T-shirt and whipped my hair about my face. One sneakered foot was propped on the dash, the other was on the hump between my floorboards and Daddy's.

He wore his usual scuffed brogans. His khaki work pants and blue work shirt had been washed to faded softness, but his hand was strong on the wheel and there was nothing faded about the cornflower blue of his eyes. His eyes narrowed now as he shook his head again over A.K.'s stupidity.

"I don't understand how come he's growed up so wild," he muttered as we crossed Possum Creek and drove along Old Forty-eight. "Less'n it's 'cause April's always made Andrew spare the rod."

"Probably genetic," I said, enjoying the rush of heavy humid air against my skin. Long as I don't have to do stoop labor in it, I don't really mind our summer weather.

"How you mean?"

"From all I hear, A.K.'s pretty much like Andrew was and he says you came near killing that peach tree down at the barn stripping off switches."

"Back then, he'd rather get a whipping than do right, that's for sure," Daddy admitted.

"And April's the one got him on the straight and narrow," I reminded him.

"Well, she ain't keeping A.K. on it."

"Can't fight the genes," I grinned.

"You throwing off on me again, girl?"

"If the shoe fits."

"I never tore up things just for the hell of it," he said mildly. "And for certain I never tore up nothing belonging to somebody else."

The sliding rear window was open and Ladybelle stuck her head in and gave my ear a lick. Blue had his head over the side, his nose to the wind. In his youth, they say, Daddy collected enough speeding tickets to paper the outhouse before they got indoor plumbing. These days he rattles around ten miles under the limit, and the dogs ambled from one side of the rusty truck bed to the other with no fear of losing their balance.

We turned onto the blacktop that led past Jimmy White's garage, crossed Forty-eight, then did a dogleg onto another blacktop, and finally wound up on the clay and gravel road that runs along Crocker land.

A narrow dirt lane leads across a field of healthy green cotton plants to where a stand of massive oaks shades a fire-blackened stone chimney. The chimney and a scattering of wild phlox among the weeds at the edge of the field are all that remain of the original Crocker homeplace.

"How'd it burn?" I asked as we bumped our way towards it.

"Chimney fire," said Daddy. (In his Colleton County

accent, it came out "chimbly far," but I had no trouble un-
derstanding him.)

"Forty year ago, it were. Martha's mama was cooking
dinner when it catched and she had to be dragged out.
Kept trying to get back in till Dwight's daddy, Cal
Bryant—he was the one got here first—he promised he'd
go back in for her milk pitcher if she'd promise to stay in
the yard. Funny what folks take a notion to save at a time
like that. Whole houseful of nice stuff and the only thing
she was worried over was a milk pitcher that maybe cost
fifty cent at Woolworth's."

"What would you save?" I asked.

"Your mama's picture," he said promptly. "The picture
albums with you young'uns. Maybe my mama's Bible if
they was time. Everything else, I could replace."

I knew what he meant even though the house was full
of irreplaceable reminders of people long gone: a hand-
pegged wardrobe that his grandfather built out of heart
pine, his mother's punched-tin pie safe that stood by the
back door, the stack of intricate hand-pieced quilts that
had warmed us through childhood's long winter nights, a
zillion bits of glass and china and tatted pillow slips and
rush-bottomed chairs and pocket knives that had been
sharpened so many times that their blades were worn
down to slender steel crescents—each object with a story,
some of which only Daddy remembered now.

Hard as it would be to lose those, losing the pictures
and the Bible would be like losing our past. Pictures can't
be retaken. And though Daddy's not much for churchgo-
ing, the Bible holds his mother's record of the family's

births and deaths and marriages in her semi-literate hand-writing.

The lane curved around the oak grove. A dusty old black two-ton truck was parked out in the cotton field near a tall magnolia tree in full bloom. As we approached, I saw that the tree stood inside a low stone wall that enclosed a small plot of ground about twenty-five feet square. The truck was fitted with a hydraulic winch to hoist slabs of marble and granite in and out of the truck's bed.

"You ever meet Rudy Peacock before?" Daddy asked as a man rose from his seat on the wall.

"Not that I remember," I said.

"His granddaddy made my daddy's stone and his daddy and him did Annie Ruth's and your mama's stone, too."

My grandfather Knott's "stone" was a ten-foot-tall black marble obelisk, erected shortly after he crashed and drowned in Possum Creek. Revenuers shot out his truck tires when he tried to outrun them with a load of his homemade whiskey. From all accounts, my grandfather was a good-hearted family man who turned to moonshining when boll weevils destroyed the cotton farms around here. It was the only way he knew to feed and clothe his extended family and pay the taxes on his little piece of land.

Daddy was barely in his teens when he became the man of the house, and defiant pride had reared that costly shaft to his father's memory long before my birth. Same with his first wife's marker, too, of course.

I probably would have met the Peacocks, father and son, when they came out to set Mother's white marble stone except that I was in full flight by then—mad at Daddy, mad at my brothers, mad at God—so mad that I stayed gone for two years.

"Rudy's right shy with women," Daddy warned as we pulled up to the big truck. "Try not to scare him."

Scare him?

The man now leaning against the truck's front fender was tall as Daddy, but so broad and muscular you could've fit two Kezzie Knotts into one Rudy Peacock's chinos and black T-shirt. Peacock's hair was granite gray and his arms were roped with veins that stood out against the muscles. He nodded politely when we were introduced, but he didn't put out his hand, his eyes didn't quite meet mine, and he soon moved back so that Daddy was a buffer between us.

Ordinarily, I'd have asked if he was the father of a Peacock girl who'd been a year or two ahead of me in high school, but he was clearly so uncomfortable that I was ready to fade into the background.

Not Daddy, though. He's always had a broad streak of mischief in him.

"Deb'rah's gonna need your vote again come election time," he said. "And won't some of your girls in school with her? What was their names, shug?"

"Now you didn't drag Mr. Peacock out here to get his vote or talk about my high school days," I said, and opened the wide iron gate set in the stone wall.

The damage was apparent as soon as I stepped inside

and it shamed and angered me that any nephew of mine had a hand in this. I can understand teenage boys buying beer illegally. I can understand why they'd come back here, well off the road and out of casual view, to drink it in the moonlight and strew the cans around. But to then start pushing over headstones? To come armed with a can of spray paint?

The need to smash and deface I do *not* understand.

I hadn't closely scrutinized the Polaroid pictures of the damage that Cyl DeGraffenried had introduced as evidence that afternoon. Mrs. Avery had picked them up, but under her disapproving eye, I had given them only a cursory, embarrassed glance. Now that I was here and could see all the girls' names printed in dark green across the stones and wall, I realized that A.K. had probably been telling the truth when he swore he hadn't used the spray can.

One hand had printed every S and every N backwards. A different hand had mixed his capitals with lowercase, then dotted each capital I. And while Andrew's son might have written his letters that way, April's son had been taught to print his alphabet perfectly long before he started kindergarten.

I've heard SBI handwriting experts say it's almost as hard for an educated person to mimic a crude writing style as it is for an uneducated person to mimic a correct style. Both groups almost always revert to true form somewhere in the document. I was pretty sure A.K. couldn't have written those backward letters that consistently. Especially not after three or four beers.

But he'd certainly had a hand in tipping over half a dozen headstones and pulling over the angel.

"No real damage to the markers," said Mr. Peacock after he'd walked around the little graveyard. "I can stand 'em back up, reseat them with a little mortar and they'll be fine as new once that latex paint's scrubbed off. Good thing they won't using oil-base."

"What about that there angel?" asked Daddy.

She was granite, not marble, about five feet tall, and she had fallen back at an angle. One wing was half-buried in the soft sandy loam, but the right wing had struck the stone wall and shattered into several chunks.

"Now that's gonna take some work," said Mr. Peacock, stroking his broad chin. "I gotta be honest with you, Mr. Kezzie. It's gonna cost. First I've got to see if what's left of that wing can take drilling."

"Drilling?" I asked.

He was so absorbed in the mechanics he forgot to be shy and actually met my eyes for a brief instant. "I'll have to put in at least two steel pins to hold the new wing tip on. Then if it's sound enough to accept the pins, I've got to see if I can match the color. Every stone's a little different, you know."

He bent down for a chunk of the broken wing that must have weighed at least fifteen pounds and hefted it in one huge hand as if it were a two-pound sack of flour. The sun had already set and daylight was fading, but we could still see the color difference between the granite's weathered surface and its freshly split interior.

His hands looked like boot leather but his touch was

delicate as his fingers gently traced the feathers chiseled on the broken stone he held, as if he were smoothing real feathers instead of granite.

"And after I match the stone, I've got to carve the feathers so they match, too."

"And if the pins won't hold or you can't match it?" asked Daddy.

"Then we'll have to make a whole new pair of wings and pin 'em on back behind the shoulder blades. By the time I give her a good buffing all over and bring her back and stand her up, they ought to look all right, but it's gonna cost you."

"Durn them boys," said Daddy, shaking his head.

"Could've been a lot worse," Peacock said. "If she'd fallen on her face, we'd have to make a whole new head. You can't never get a new nose to look exactly right."

As they continued to talk, I wandered around in the twilight to read the names of Crockers long gone. Old Mr. Ham Crocker had been eighty-eight. His sister Florence, laid to rest here around the turn of the century, "died a maid of 14 yrs., 3 mos., 24 days." And there was Daddy's great-uncle Yancy Knott "and also his beloved wife Lulalia Crocker Knott," both dead of typhoid in 1902.

Gardenia bushes had been planted on either side of the gate and they were in full bloom. Their heavy sweet fragrance filled the air and hummingbird moths were busily working the fleshy white blossoms.

Lightning bugs drifted on the still June air. Mosquitoes, too, I realized, and slapped at one that was biting my arm.

Suddenly the quiet evening was interrupted by a pager on Rudy Peacock's belt. He squinted at the tiny screen in the failing light, then strode across the cemetery to his truck, pulled out a cell phone and punched in some numbers.

"Where?" we heard him ask urgently. The next minute he was stepping up into the cab.

"Sorry, Mr. Kezzie, Miss Deb'rah, but I got to go. I'm on the volunteer fire department and we just got a call-out. Sounds pretty bad."

"Where?" asked Daddy, his long legs covering the ground between them.

Already we could hear sirens on the other side of the woods.

"Starling's Crossroads," said Rudy Peacock as he swung himself into the seat and switched on the flashing red light suctioned to his dashboard. "The church yonder."

❧ 6 ❧

Storm Alert! Isaiah 29:6
—Pleasant Grove Freewill Baptist

"It must be Balm of Gilead," I said as we sped through the lane behind Rudy Peacock. "Where that Mr. Freeman preaches."

"Yep," said Daddy.

Despite the warm evening, we had the pickup windows rolled tight to keep from breathing in the clouds of dust Peacock's truck was kicking up. It was like driving through fog and Daddy kept his beams on low so he could see the way.

When we reached the blacktop, our windows came down and we heard sirens converging from all directions. We followed as Mr. Peacock made another quick turn onto a clay road with deep, sunbaked ruts that hadn't been scraped since the last heavy rain. A car was ahead of him and another turned in behind us. The red clay made it even dustier than the lane we'd just come from, and at that speed we were jounced around so hard that we had to shout to hear each other. Between rising dust and falling darkness, it was hard to make out the old converted gas station until we were right on it and could see the front lit up in kaleidoscopic flashes from the red lights in a couple of volunteers' pickup trucks.

Flames were already jetting through the back left corner of the roof and Daddy pulled in behind Peacock just as the West Colleton volunteer fire truck swung in next to the building itself.

Ignoring Daddy's command to stay in the truck, I jumped out to see if I could help salvage anything from inside.

Like hundreds of small two-pump gas stations built in the 1940s, this one had the usual low-pitched A-line roof that extended out over a narrow pull-through to cover the gas pumps plus a smaller pump for kerosene, none of which was still here.

A fireman called out, "Reckon they's still any gas in them old tanks?" and I hoped Daddy had heard and that he'd stand well back in case something set off the tanks that were probably still there beneath the ground.

Two barred windows flanked the center door, and I followed a burly volunteer in protective gear into the large open space once lined with shelves of canned goods, sugar, flour and cereal, with room for a counter to one side, a drink box at the front and a potbellied stove in the middle. A narrow door at the rear would have provided cross-ventilation in summer.

Now the single room held ten or twelve long wooden pews, an old-fashioned upright piano and a homemade wooden pulpit, and the cross-ventilation fed the flames blazing in the far left corner. I saw that one of the pews was ablaze on its own in the middle of the room, but what with the heavy pulpit Bible and grabbing up anything else I could lay my hands on, I was too busy to think just then what that might mean.

"Get out! Get out! Get out!" cried the man with the pulpit on his shoulders, but there were hymn books scattered along the pews—how could this impoverished congregation buy new ones? And fans. No air-conditioning here—I had to save the fans. Sparks showered down, stinging my bare arms.

Gasping for air, choking on smoke, I heaped hymnals and fans on top of the huge pulpit Bible and stumbled through the door just as rafters began to crash down behind me.

I was no sooner out into the fresh air than Daddy grabbed me roughly as if I were ten years old again and he meant to shake some sense into me.

"Don't you never do nothing like that again as long as you live," he raged as he brushed at the singed places where burning sparks had fallen onto my hair.

Between coughs to clear my lungs and trying to assure him that I wasn't hurt, I almost didn't see those ugly words spray-painted in dark green across the front of the white clapboard structure.

As soon as I did see them though, I knew that this was no accidental electrical fire. Those letters were too similar to the ones sprayed across the Crocker family cemetery. And while I still didn't think A.K. had written either set, I could only pray that he'd spent the evening repenting in his room tonight and that he hadn't stepped foot out of the house since he got home from court—that he hadn't been out with any racist friends.

"Back! Get back!" shouted the young man who'd rescued the pulpit. He was sweating profusely inside his heavy fire suit, but his eyes flashed with excitement as he ordered us further away. The interior was now such a fiery furnace that even Shadrach, Meshach and Abednego couldn't have rescued anything else from its depths.

The rear of the building suddenly sagged and the rusty tin roof crashed in with sharp creaks and bangs. Geysers of sparks shot up twenty feet or more into the night sky, and the old dry wood beneath the tin burned like heart pine lightwood. Rafters pulled loose from their nails and sheets of tin buckled in the heat as more oxygen fed the flames. Clearly there was no saving any of the building and now the firemen turned their efforts to confining the fire to the structure itself as they drenched the scorched trees and bushes around the edges to keep them from catching.

There was nothing to do but stand and watch it burn to the ground.

More cars and trucks had pulled in, several of the arrivals members of this small congregation. Tears trickled down the face of a gray-haired black woman as she filmed the blaze with her video camera, but there were angry mutterings from others of the men and women standing apart from us whites.

❧ 7 ❧

Some things have to be believed to be seen.
—Park Methodist Church

The fire was still smoldering when we left and the fire truck was packing up its gear, but people continued to arrive as word spread through the black community. One of the deacons took the big pulpit Bible from me and he thanked me for rescuing it. His wife smoothed the white lace runner. "My grandmother crocheted this when I was a little girl. Thank Jesus, you saved it."

Another member of the congregation smiled when she saw those stick-and-cardboard giveaway fans. "You don't mean to say you walked through fire for these raggedy old things, do you?"

"You just grab up whatever you see at a time like that," I said, feeling as foolish as old Mrs. Crocker must have felt once the emergency was past and she realized she'd risked a neighbor's life for a fifty-cent milk pitcher.

"I hope you ain't going to make a habit of that," Daddy said gruffly as we walked back to the truck.

"No, sir," I said and squeezed his work-rough hand in mine.

Neither of us had much to say as we drove home through the warm still night. The odor of smoke was on us both and every time I touched my hair where sparks had landed, a singed-feathers smell reached my nose. I wasn't looking forward to seeing the damage in a mirror.

When we came to Old Forty-eight, Daddy turned in to a farm lane that led past Jap Stancil's old house. It was dark and deserted, though there was a light on up at his daughter-in-law's house where she still waited trial for shooting Mr. Jap's son.

A half-moon was up and the air was full of the summer sounds of frogs and cicadas and crickets. We crossed Possum Creek onto Knott land over a homemade bridge of logs and boards, then took a west-branching lane that led past a twenty-acre tobacco field. It must have been topped that afternoon, for the smell of green tobacco was strong on the air and wilted pink blossoms littered the ground between the rows.

We came up to Andrew's house from the rear and his rabbit dogs announced our coming. By the time Daddy pulled into the yard and cut off his motor, my brother had turned on the back porch light and was standing there waiting for us, barefooted and shirtless.

It wasn't much past ten o'clock, but most farmers are up at first light during barning time. Andrew yelled at the dogs and they hushed barking before I had my door open.

"Something wrong?" he asked.

"Where's A.K.?" said Daddy.

"In bed, I reckon. Why?"

"You want to wake him up?"

Of all the boys, Andrew's the one who favors Daddy the most, especially now that streaks of gray are appearing in his thick dark hair. He nodded curtly and stepped back into the house.

Daddy flicked one of those wooden kitchen matches with his thumbnail to light his cigarette and I smelled the familiar pungent blend of sulphur and tobacco smoke that always conjures up a hundred random memories. Into the silence came the lonesome call of a chuck-will's-widow from the woods down by the barns. That lopsided moon was caught in the branches of the pecan trees beyond the pumphouse.

Several minutes later, a sleepy A.K. stumbled out to the porch in his underwear, all arms and gangly legs now, but a man's height and starting to fill out. "Granddaddy?"

"Where was you this evening, boy?" His voice was stern.

"Right here." A.K. glanced uneasily at his father, who took a seat on the edge of the porch. "I been grounded till August."

"You didn't sneak out somewhere?"

"No, sir."

"Talk on the phone with them two friends of your'n?"

"I might've with Raymond Bagwell for a minute."

Andrew gave him a sharp look. "Didn't you hear me say I didn't want y'all talking together anytime soon?"

"That's why I called him," A.K. said sullenly. "I needed to tell him not to call over here for a while."

" 'Bout what time was that?" asked Daddy.

A.K. shrugged. "Right after supper. Around seven maybe? *Jeopardy* was just coming on."

"What's happened?" asked April, pushing open the screen door and joining us on the porch. Her short sandy brown hair stood up in tufts because she was forever running her fingers through it when worried or distracted. She has a small neat body and good legs, but I knew that she wore that oversized T-shirt because middle age was thickening her waist in spite of all she could do to stop it. "Is it more trouble?"

"Somebody set fire tonight to that colored church over at Starling's Crossroads," Daddy said.

A.K. straightened indignantly. "*Me?* You asking if *I* did it? You think I'd do a thing like that?"

"Didn't think you'd tear up a graveyard neither," Daddy said mildly.

"There!" said Andrew. "Now you see what I mean? Once you lose your good name, you don't get it back just because you say you're sorry."

April nudged him with the toe of her sneaker and he subsided.

"Who did most of the spray-painting at the graveyard?" I asked A.K. "Raymond or Charles?"

"They was both about equal." ("*Were* both," April murmured.) "Why?"

"Because there was writing at the church, too, and it

A man's heart deviseth the way,
But the Lord directeth his steps.
—Riverview Methodist

The fire—now called the "burning"—made the late news that night. It also led the seven o'clock news the next morning as I was stoically resisting Aunt Zell's hot buttered biscuits and breakfasting on an unbuttered English muffin and black coffee. (If they don't hurry up and finish my house, I'm not going to fit through the door frame.)

Not surprisingly, every channel carried a call for federal investigators by a certain leading black activist, North Carolina's answer to Jesse Jackson. Wallace Adderly had put himself in the news so much that most people were familiar with the sketchy outlines of his history.

Born on the wrong side of the river in Wilmington, Wallace Adderly joined NOISE (the National Organization In Search of Equality) in the late sixties when membership was both politically effective and majorly cool. NOISE was a splinter group of the Student Non-Violent Coordinating Committee and was less violent than the

Black Panthers, but more confrontational than CORE (Congress for Racial Equality). He and his cohorts criss-crossed the South, popping up in odd places to encourage voter registration drives, to protest unsafe working condi-tions, to harass segregated hotels and restaurants. Early on, he was charged with leading an unsanctioned protest march that turned into a riot. The judge offered to dismiss the case if he'd resign from NOISE.

"I'll quit NOISE the day you quit Willow Lodge," Adderly said defiantly, naming the segregated country club that was the stronghold of white male privilege in Wilmington.

The judge slapped him with contempt of court.

Sometime in the mid-seventies though, Adderly grew disillusioned with the NOISE leadership. On his own, he abruptly dropped out and, in his words, turned bourgeois, graduating cum laude from UNC-Wilmington. He ranked first in his law class at NC Central and aced the state bar exam on his first try.

Not that he automatically got his license to practice right away.

In view of his clashes with the law during his activist days, the board of examiners felt duty bound to conduct a hearing on his moral fitness. I've heard that certain Re-publican attorneys tried to influence the board to withhold his license because of his prison record, but the board ruled that most of his jail time stemmed from sassing judges and that the rest had been imposed for his attempts to eradicate racial discrimination. Two days after gaining his license, he opened a practice down in Wilmington.

Only he doesn't always stay in Wilmington.

Turning "bourgeois" has made him comfortably middle class but it hasn't banked his fires. He still does a lot of pro bonos and whenever a high-profile case with racist implications rears its head anywhere in the state, a call goes out for Wallace Adderly. At forty-something, he's telegenic, quick-witted and politically savvy, and there are many who thought he should be running against Jesse Helms this time instead of Harvey Gantt.

That's why I wasn't surprised to see his face on every news channel that morning. The burning of a black church made it more than a local crime and the larger issues it symbolized would move it out of our local jurisdiction. I knew I'd soon be seeing some of my ATF pals on TV as well.

DA Douglas Woodall was shown on the scene and his voice was serious as he assured Channel 11's Greg Barnes, "Our office is going to look very closely at all surrounding circumstances."

Doug never overlooks any circumstances—or angles either, for that matter. The assistant he'd chosen to accompany him out to Balm of Gilead this morning was Cyl DeGraffenried, very photogenic and very black.

Sheriff Bo Poole was out there, too, with both black deputies, and he promised his department's full cooperation, "But, Greg, I'd like to caution everybody about jumping to conclusions. We should remember that the preliminary findings of the president's task force on church arsons indicate that most of these fires are set by individuals acting alone and not by members of hate groups."

"Hate is hate, whether expressed by a group or an individual acting alone," said Wallace Adderly, "and whatever the motive, it's a black congregation hurting out here this morning."

Channel 5 had obtained a copy of the amateur videotape I saw being filmed last night. It was fuzzy and the bright flames washed out a lot of details. You could make out a swastika and two K's, but the letters looked black against the fire, not the green I knew them to be.

This morning, there was only the stump of the utility pole, smoldering ashes and twisted tin. Up above in the background, you could see the cars on I-40 slow down to rubberneck at the two news vans parked down by the dead end. Channel 11's cameras panned around the grounds, lingering on some of the black faces fixed in pain and anger, then stopped on the Reverend Ralph Freeman.

When asked to speculate about the mind-set of the arsonist, he shook his head. "I'm afraid I'm too new to this community to know who the haters are. What lifts my spirits are the offers of help that are already pouring in, the support of the good people in this area."

The camera caught Cyl DeGraffenried off guard with one eyebrow skeptically raised.

"Oh, look," said Aunt Zell. "Isn't that Frances Turner's boy Donny?"

I know the Turners only by name, but as the camera panned across the official faces, I caught a glimpse of a stocky young white man and recognized him from last night.

"He's the one who carried out the pulpit on his shoulder," I said, pouring myself another cup of coffee as the station went to a commercial for orange juice.

"Oh, he's strong all right." Aunt Zell held out her own cup and I topped it for her. "They used to call him Tank when he was a little boy."

"He's still a tank," I said. "He hoisted that pulpit as if it was a chair."

"Frances says he works out with weights down at the fire station. It's really good of so many young men to give up their free time like that, don't you think? It just goes to show you, doesn't it?"

"Doesn't what?" I asked, not following her.

"The Turner boy. When you think of how prejudiced he is."

"Is he?"

"Frances says ever since high school when he lost a wrestling championship because the black boy he was wrestling with cheated. Or so he told Frances. Of course, Frances—she's a little prejudiced, too, though she claims not to be. But prejudiced or not, Donny did do what he could last night to save a black church, didn't he?"

I nodded.

"Just goes to prove how bigotry can fly out the window when people need help. Shows real dedication to a higher ideal, don't you think? But Frances, she worries he's so dedicated he doesn't have time for girlfriends."

This from my aunt who's active in at least a half-dozen volunteer organizations and still manages to find lots of time to keep Uncle Ash happy.

* * *

As the news moved on to other stories around the area, Aunt Zell clicked her tongue. "You don't suppose those Shop-Mark people had anything to do with it, do you?"

"Shop-Mark?" I was clueless as to why she'd link the South's biggest chain of upscale discount stores to a poor country church on the backside of nowhere.

"But it's not nowhere anymore," said Aunt Zell. "Haven't you heard? They're going to build a new exit ramp off I-40 to accommodate all the growth over there. Ash's sister Agnes? Her son's on the Highway Commission. That whole corridor between I-40 and New Forty-eight's going to be developed. And Shop-Mark's buying up land there at Starling's Crossroads. Agnes says it's going to be the biggest Shop-Mark between Washington and Atlanta."

"So that's what Maidie meant," I said.

Aunt Zell gave me an inquiring look.

"Last night when we were washing dishes, she said that Balm of Gilead had called Mr. Freeman to their pulpit because he'd seen his last church through a big building program. Even if the land jumps in price though, how much can they get for that little bit of ground?"

"But it's not just the churchyard," Aunt Zell said. "I heard it was more like eight or nine acres."

Eight or nine acres in the middle of an area slated for heavy development? That would certainly be enough for a hefty down payment on a new church building.

I wondered if the old building was insured.

❧ 9 ❧

Are you helping men to heaven or hell?
—Highland Baptist Church

The edginess that hung over the courthouse that morning had less to do with June's smothering heat and humidity than with Channel 5's news van parked out front. *News and Observer* and *Ledger* reporters roamed the halls and sidewalks, too, looking for man-in-the-street reactions to the destruction of a black church. Although it's glossed over now and goes pretty much unmentioned when people talk about the good old days, Dobbs is still the town that used to greet its visitors with a huge billboard that pictured nightriders, a burning cross and big letters that said, "Welcome to Klan Kuntry!"

As a child standing behind the driver's seat when Mother and I drove over to Dobbs to visit Aunt Zell, I'd been offended by the sign. Not because of what it stood for—to a seven-year-old raised up Baptist, one cross looks pretty much like another and I had no idea what the Klan was. But I did know that "Kuntry" was bad spelling.

"How come they don't fix it right?" I'd ask Mother.

" 'Cause they're dumber than dirt," Mother would always answer.

I'm not saying these reporters were necessarily looking to find a white hood sticking out from under the bill of a man-in-the-street's John Deere cap, but a couple of snarling, dumber-than-dirt rednecks would have goosed up the ain't-no-racists-here protestations, which was all they were getting on tape.

Dwight Bryant, the deputy sheriff I've known since I was in diapers, had a sour look on his face when he stopped past the broom closet that serves as my bare-basics office when I'm sitting court in Dobbs. "Ed Gardner's looking for you."

I didn't play innocent. Ed used to be part of the Friday night crowd at Miss Molly's on South Wilmington Street when Terry Wilson and I were hanging together three or four years ago. Terry's State Bureau of Investigation; Ed's federal: Alcohol, Tobacco and Firearms. These days, "Firearms" includes any incendiary device that results in an explosion or a fire. Colleton County's old rundown tobacco warehouses have a bad habit of catching fire in the middle of the night around here, so we get to see a little more of Ed than other folks might.

"I'm always happy to talk to him," I said, "but don't you and Bo want to know what I saw, too?"

He shrugged unhappily and I almost got up to pat his shoulder like one of my brothers when they were down. In age, Dwight's somewhere between Will and the little twins and might as well have been another brother, since he hung out with them so much. Kidd Chapin may be a hair taller, but Dwight's more muscular and solid, like my brothers by Daddy's first wife. At times I feel as protective of him as if he really was one of my brothers.

"A little territorial infighting going on here?" I asked sympathetically.

"Aw, you know how it is. The Feds are polite, but they don't think we know squat. And I'm stuck hanging around, waiting for Buster Cavanaugh to get here and ride out there with me." He gave a rueful grin. "'Course, old Buster now, he *don't* know squat."

Fire Marshall in Colleton County's always been more of an honorary term than a working title and Buster probably knows less about an arson investigation than I do. But he was connected to a couple of the county commissioners and he'd have his nose out of joint if he didn't get included in the day's festivities. He never misses a chance to slap that magnetic Fire Marshall sign onto the side of his car and turn on his flashing red light.

Absently, I touched the little blisters scattered on my forearm.

"Hurt much?" Dwight asked.

I shook my head and pulled down the sleeve of my robe. "Looks worse than it is. At least my hair doesn't still smell like singed chicken feathers."

"I hear Mr. Kezzie wasn't real happy about you running into that church last night for a handful of cardboard fans."

"I saved more than fans," I said indignantly. "I brought out the pulpit Bible and—"

Dwight's lips were twitching. Done it to me again.

I let him laugh, then said, "Be better if you'd heard who did it."

According to my watch, court was due to convene in two minutes and, as I stood up, Dwight turned serious. "Look like arson to you?"

" 'Fraid so. When I got inside, the worst was over in the corner where the electric wires came in, but one of the pews in the middle of the room was burning, too, and it was nowhere near a wire."

Dwight opened the door for me and walked me down the hall. "You reckon it really was a hate burning or just kids fooling around?"

"Who knows?" I paused at the door to my courtroom. "But it sure did look a lot like what was done out at the Crocker cemetery—green paint, block printing, swastikas. I'm no handwriting expert though. You need to get Cyl DeGraffenried to show you the Polaroids."

"You saying *A.K.'s* involved in this?"

"A.K. didn't do any spray-painting at the cemetery," I said firmly. "Andrew and April both say he was home last night and I didn't see either of his friends. Besides, don't arsonists usually like to hang around and watch their handiwork?"

"I heard that Starling's a racist."

"But why would he take his anger out on a church?"

"Because it's at Starling's Crossroads? And he already used green paint one time this week, right?"

I nodded glumly. "But it still might just be a coincidence."

Dwight pushed open the courtroom door and stood back for me to enter.

"All rise," said the bailiff as soon as he caught sight of me. "Oyez, oyez, oyez. This honorable court for the County of Colleton is now open and sitting for the dispatch of its business. God save the state and this honorable court, the Honorable Judge Deborah Knott presiding. Be seated."

Normally Cyl DeGraffenried is already standing when I walk in. Today, the bailiff was halfway through his spiel before the words seemed to register enough to bring her to her feet. Reid was defending a young Hispanic for possession of marijuana and when he requested that the case be thrown out because of sloppy police mistakes with the search warrant, her opposing argument was so unfocussed that I granted Reid's request and dismissed the charges.

Cyl didn't even shrug, just called the next case in an absent-minded voice. We were almost to the midmorning recess before she got herself up to speed. By noon, she was again demanding heads on a silver salver but somehow her heart didn't seem to be in it.

"Left it a little late, ain't you?" asked Leamon Webb, who runs the Print Place down from the courthouse in Dobbs, when I stopped in on my noon recess. "Judge Longmire had his campaign stuff printed up in February."

"That's because he had a challenger in the May primary," I said, feeling a little testy.

I told myself it was still only June. Plenty of time till the November election and it's not like I have any serious competition this year. ("*Not as if,*" came Aunt Zell's schoolteacher voice in my head.)

Everybody's a critic these days. First Minnie, who wanted to know if I was getting complacent; then my niece Emma, who was busy putting stuff together for Vacation Bible School; and now Leamon.

Minnie's my sister-in-law and campaign adviser and Emma's the family computer whiz who gets saddled with any electronically creative project her relatives can think up, so I'm obliged to listen to them grumble. But Leamon Webb's not one drop of kin and there are other print shops in the county. Besides, I hadn't eaten lunch yet and I didn't have time for any hassle.

"If you're too backed up to do it—" I reached for the folder with Emma's camera-ready sheets that lay on the counter between us.

"Naw, now, I didn't say that."

Leamon slid the folder out from under my hand and looked at the mock-ups my niece had done of a simple single-fold leaflet and pasteboard bookmarks. Both had a dignified head-and-shoulders picture of me in my judge's robes and "RE-ELECT JUDGE KNOTT" in bold block capitals. In the picture, the lacy edge of a standup white collar was meant to remind voters that I was both feminine and womanly. My shoulder-length dark blonde hair was pinned up in a modified French twist to make me look more mature and my blue eyes looked candidly into the camera. The bookmark stated my background and experience—the legal and professional bits, *not* the personal, thank you very much.

Because I'm only thirty-six and haven't sat on many boards or commissions, the leaflet encompassed lots of tasteful, if useless, white space. A short text elaborated that I'd begun my law studies at Columbia and finished at Chapel Hill and that I'd been a partner in the well-respected firm of Lee and Stephenson right here in Colleton County. It also mentioned that I was a member of First Baptist of Dobbs and that I'd been born near Cotton Grove, smack-dab in the middle of Judicial Court District 11-C.

It did not mention a disastrous attempt at marriage, my lack of husband and 1.3 children (the county average in my socioeconomic age group), nor that my father had once run white lightning from Canada to Mexico.

I didn't expect anyone else to mention those last three things either, since Howard Woodlief was my only opposition this time and judgeships aren't hotly contested before statewide television cameras. Mine was nothing like the race shaping up between Richard Petty and Elaine Marshall for Secretary of State. Even CNN was interested in that one, since she would be the first woman elected to North Carolina's Council of State if she won, while King Richard would be its first NASCAR champion if he took the checkered flag.

Then there was the Jesse Helms/Harvey Gantt rematch.

With all those horses crashing through the woods, my run for reelection would be lucky to get a mention in the Dobbs *Ledger.*

Which was why I needed bookmarks and leaflets to remind the voters I'd be on the ballot.

Leamon's lips moved as he read to himself the closing motto that Emma had composed: "Caring, Compassionate and Competent."

Emma loves alliteration.

So do most of the voters in this district.

"Real nice," said Leamon. "Now was you thinking black ink on white or can we juice it up with a little color?"

With no time left for a sit-down lunch, I grabbed a salad and a bottle of apple juice at the sandwich shop across the street and carried them back to the courthouse, intending to eat at my desk. But when I tried to open the office door, it was locked.

Odd. I never push the button latch when I leave because I've never had a key. No problem though. Luther Parker, who shares the connecting lavatory, wasn't back yet, so I scooted across his office, through the lavatory, then stopped short as I opened the inner door.

Cyl DeGraffenried was there, hunched in the chair before my desk.

She whirled around to face me.

"Sorry," she said. "I thought you were— I needed a little privacy— I—I—"

Her hair was disheveled and as she stood up, it was clear from her swollen eyes that she'd been crying. Indeed a last tear trickled slowly down her smooth dark cheek as she stood there staring at me helplessly. In the time that I've known her, I've never seen Cyl DeGraffen-ried cry or look helpless and it left me at a loss, too.

"That's okay." I gestured awkwardly with my brown paper bag and started to back out. "I'll eat at Luther's desk. You take all the time you want."

I retreated to Luther's office and a few minutes later heard water running in the lavatory sink. I was halfway through my salad when she opened the door.

Cold compresses had worked magic on her eyes and every hair was in place. I could almost swear that she'd even sent her beige linen suit out for a quick press.

"You okay?" I asked.

"I'm fine. And I apologize for inconveniencing you."

Not only was every hair in place, so were all her defenses.

"You didn't inconvenience me." I unscrewed the top of my juice bottle. "Apple juice? There are cups—"

"No, thank you," she said brusquely, heading for the door.

"Look, Cyl," I said. "Is there anything I can do? Would it help to talk?"

"To *you*?" There was so much scorn in her voice that I felt as if I'd been slapped.

"Why not me?" I asked indignantly just as Luther Parker opened the door.

"Excuse me," said Cyl, and Luther stepped back to let her pass.

His chocolate-brown eyes moved from Cyl's disappearing back to my usurpation of his desk.

"Something going on I should know about?"

"What's her real problem, Luther?" I asked him bluntly.

He looked at me over his rimless glasses. "You mean right now or in general?"

"Either one."

He shrugged. "Beats me. But then I've always lived in Makely, so how would I know? My wife knew her when she was a kid, though."

I was confused, knowing that Cyl grew up down near New Bern. "Really? Louise has down east connections?"

"No, but Ms. DeGraffenried has Cotton Grove connections. When she first started working for Woodall, I remember Louise said something about seeing her at church with her auntie or granny or somebody when she was just a little girl."

Louise Parker's great-great-grandfather had been Mount Olive's first black preacher and, according to Maidie, she's never moved her membership over to Makely even though she and Luther must be married at least thirty years.

"Was Cyl wired this tight back then?" I wondered aloud. "Is that why she grew up and turned into a Republican?"

Luther's big dark face crinkled with laughter. "You say Republican like some people say Satan. Democrats have no monopoly on virtue, Deborah, and this is a yellowdog, big D Democrat saying it to you."

"Who said anything about virtue?" I asked.

❧ 10 ❧

Never let a bleak past
Cloud a bright future
—Barbecue Church

When I came down the hot marble steps of the courthouse that afternoon, Ed Gardner was sitting on a green slatted bench beneath the magnolia tree that shades our memorial to those Colleton County boys who died in the First World War.

A bronze doughboy in khaki leggings and campaign cap holds a carbine at the ready and squints into the sunset. He's as feisty as the Confederate general rising in the stirrups as his fire-breathing stallion plunges into battle on the other side of the courthouse. World War II's monument is a tall slab of white marble with the names of our dead in brass letters. Daddy's brother Pat's name is on that one.

None of my eleven brothers were old enough for Korea, but Frank was a machinist mate with the Sixth Fleet in the Far East during Vietnam. He wound up making a career out of the Navy and has now retired to San Diego. One of the lucky ones.

"Ever notice anything odd about monument horses?" Ed asked as he ambled toward me.

Smiling, I said, "The fact that they're usually well-endowed stallions and almost never geldings or mares? Yeah, I've noticed."

He crushed out his cigarette and buried the butt in the border of bright yellow marigolds that lined the walk. "Must've played hell with battle formations every time a couple of mares went into heat."

I laughed. "Wonder how many lieutenants got busted to corporal because their mares led a general's stallion astray?"

"We'll never know," said Ed. "They always leave the good stuff out of the history books."

He glanced up at my high-heeled white sandals. "I was gonna ask you if you had time to take a walk along the river, but those shoes aren't made for dirt, are they?"

In times past, we'd have automatically headed straight for the lounge at the Holiday Inn where you can drink and smoke, but Ed's quit drinking and cigarettes aren't welcome at most alcohol-free places these days, even in North Carolina. Besides, it was a nice day. Hot, of course, but at least a breeze was blowing.

"Dirt's no problem" I said. "I keep a pair of sneakers in my car."

We crossed the street to the parking lot, catching up on gossip as we went. I asked about his wife, Linda ("She's doing good, just working too hard"), he asked about Kidd

("Doing just fine"), and we both agreed it was too bad we didn't see much of each other now that neither of us hung out at Miss Molly's anymore. I changed shoes, locked my purse in the trunk of the car and stuck the keys in the pocket of my beige and white coatdress.

From the parking lot, it was only a short walk to one of the steps that led from the adjacent street down to the town commons. There's a scattering of benches and picnic tables and some grassy play areas where you first enter, then paths meander off along the riverbank through clumps of azaleas. The azaleas had finished blooming, but butterfly bushes made colorful splashes of purple, yellow or white, and swallowtail butterflies floated from one to another as we passed.

Ed's eight or ten years older, so gray hairs are popping out on his brown head and in the closely cropped brown beard that softens a jutting chinline. A couple of inches taller than I, he's compactly built and gives off the vibes of a tightly wound spring. As usual, he wore a short-sleeved cotton shirt—today's was brown checks with white buttons—jeans and scuffed brown boots that looked as if they'd been walking on charred wet ashes.

"You just come from Balm of Gilead?" I asked.

"What's left of it. Which is damn little."

"Enough to draw any conclusions?"

He paused to light a cigarette and moved around to the other side so the breeze could carry his smoke away from me. (Ed's more of a gentleman than he likes to admit.)

"You mean did the dog find accelerant and track the

gas can back to the Amoco station where the bad guy bought five gallons with his own charge card? No."

"But you did find gasoline residue?"

"Well, Sparky was wagging his tail like it was gas and it smelled like gas to me, too, but we'll have to wait and run it through the lab first." He took a deep drag and exhaled twin jets of smoke through his nostrils. "Tell me about your nephew and his little friends."

"A.K.'s not part of this," I said. "He hasn't been out from under his parents' noses since last weekend."

"You sure about that?"

"A.K. might lie to my daddy, but Andrew and April never would."

Ed grinned. He knows the legends some of his older revenuer friends have told about Daddy. "Then tell me about his friends."

Again I shook my head. "I really don't know them. I heard that the Starling boy's family used to own the land that the church stood on, but that was back probably before he was even born. As for Raymond Bagwell, all I know is that one of my old high school teachers thinks he's a fine young man that Starling's led astray."

With the edge of his boot, Ed scraped out a small hole, dropped his cigarette butt into it, then tamped the dirt back over it. "You get a good look at the words painted on the church wall?"

"Pretty good. And before you ask, yes, it looked like the same color green paint and I suppose they could've been lettered by one of those boys. Can't you compare the two?"

He shook his head. "There's not enough on that video-tape to go to court with. All we've got's part of a KKK and a swastika. Your brother alibis your nephew, Bagwell and Starling alibi each other—any fifty-dollar lawyer could argue that the angle distorts the letters or that the paint is black, not green. If there'd been even a smear left, we could've tried matching it to what I hear was used in the cemetery."

I told him about the one pew burning in the middle of the church, well away from the primary fire and he rolled his eyes scornfully. "Amateurs."

We'd reached the end of the main path. From here, it dwindled into a true hiking trail, one person wide, through a tangle of briars, trumpet vines, birches and wax myrtles.

As we turned to go back, Ed said, "Any of your kin-folks on the volunteer fire department?"

"No," I said. "Why?"

"I was thinking that if they were, they might have no-ticed something and mentioned it to you."

"You kidding? All those guys were noticing last night was how quick they could get water on the fire and how much they could save. They were running on adrenaline," I said and told him about the way the Turner boy had hoisted that big wooden pulpit as if it were no heavier than a toothpick. "I doubt they were looking for clues first thing."

"Turner?" asked Ed. "Donny Turner?"

"You know him?"

"I've heard of him," he answered slowly. "Big guy? Never misses a call-out?"

"Big, yes," I said. "But you'd have to ask somebody else about his dedication. He certainly seemed to have his heart in it last night. Not to mention his back."

Abruptly changing the subject, Ed said, "You sit in a courtroom every day. See much racially motivated stuff?"

"An occasional barroom brawl," I answered promptly. "And sometimes a high school scuffle will get out of hand. Or someone will file a civil suit claiming they were either fired or not hired because of race."

I thought about the people I'd gone to high school with, both white and black. Most of them married now, most of them with children of their own and settled into some sort of nine-to-five job. Most of them decent human beings.

Most of them. Not all.

There are very few of us who don't have bits and pieces of covert racism embedded in our psyches. Things that pop out when we aren't expecting it, the "what else can you expect from a [insert ethnic or racist epithet of choice]?" Things we're usually too ashamed to express, the very things we act superior about when our nearest and dearest do express them.

"We're probably always going to have rednecks who don't have anything but their white skins to feel superior about and shiftless blacks who think they're totally enti-tled because their ancestors were once slaves. For the most part though, whatever their bedrock feelings may be, I think most people around here try to keep a civil tongue and get on with their own business."

Ed lit another cigarette as I searched for the right words.

"I guess what I'm saying is that I've never felt we were so polarized here in Colleton County that we'd have hate burnings like last night. You're going to find it was a kid acting out, doing it more for kicks than for hatred. You just wait and see. I'm sure you are."

I didn't realize I was getting so vehement till Ed held up his hands in surrender. "Hey, you don't have to convince me. One thing though: this volunteer fire department. Any blacks on it?"

"You saying you don't think they came out as fast as they would've for a white church?" I snapped.

"Don't be so touchy. I'm just trying to see the big picture here."

We came up the steps beside the fenced-in play yard of a church-sponsored daycare center. Under the watchful eye of two white women, little children were swinging, playing in the sandbox, hanging from monkey bars—black kids, white kids, even a couple of kids of Asian descent.

Surely it was going to be different for them?

Burden Drop-Off Center (Matthew 11:28)
—New Testament Baptist Church

Next day, Friday, things were a little quieter. Ed and his people had nothing to say on record, the television cameras and reporters drifted back to Raleigh, the county commissioners were talking about appointing an interracial task force, and Wallace Adderly had been invited (invited himself?) to speak at the interchurch fellowship meeting that was still scheduled for Sunday at Mount Olive.

My calendar was so light that I was finished by two, which suited me just fine. I didn't want to be anywhere around when A.K. checked into jail at six. Andrew, who actually spent a night or three in the old jail back when he was doggedly climbing Fool's Hill himself, had sounded stoical when I called last night, but April's seen too many prison movies. She was terrified that A.K. was going to be raped or beaten up and nothing I said could convince her that things like that didn't happen in our new jailhouse.

For all I knew, she was probably planning to come along and camp out in Gwen Utley's office for the whole forty-eight hours. Gwen's one of our magistrates and her door's on the same basement hallway as the jail. Gwen's pretty no-nonsense though, so maybe *she* could reassure April.

On the way out of town, I stopped past Aunt Zell's where I've lived for the last few years and changed into sneakers, a faded red cotton T-shirt and my favorite pair of cutoffs. A baseball cap and work gloves and I was ready to head out to the farm to see what the builders had done since I last had a chance to look.

My brother Adam out in California had sent me a book with several passive solar house plans and the modest one I'd picked had a concrete slab floor, steel framing, a tiny sunroom and a couple of strategically placed masonry walls to store heat in cold weather. South-facing windows would catch the low winter sun, while the eaves were angled to block most of the higher summer sun. A trellis of wisteria would help shade the south side until the trees got taller, and extra thick insulation would cut down on both heating and cooling costs without adding too much to the overall building cost.

The two solar collectors on the roof and the hot water tank were a bigger investment, but I liked the idea of letting the sun heat my water from March till November.

"And if you'd ante up another ten or fifteen thou, you could go totally off-grid," Adam says, e-mailing me diagrams and figures about storage batteries, photovoltaics, and Swedish refrigerators. This from a man who enjoys the Silicon Valley lifestyle in a seven-thousand-square-foot house.

"Hey, I use solar energy to heat the pool," he says indignantly.

It was another hot and sticky day here in eastern North Carolina, but I kept my car windows down and the air conditioner off. If I hoped to do any work on the house, it would seem even hotter to step out of a cool car into ninety-two degrees.

A church sign on the way out of town read

> *God's fire in your heart*
> *Will keep you from burning.*

Okay.

Churches have always had signs, of course. Usually they're dignified brick boxes neatly lettered on either side with the name of the pastor and the hours of service. In the last few years though, the brick boxes started having a little glass door on either side and a signboard inside that spells out exhortational messages with changeable letters.

Or else the pastors use one of those portable signs on wheels, the kind that usually have a big red arrow pointing to a used car sale: "All prices slashed!!"

Not all the church messages make good sense—especially when some of the letters fall off and you have to guess at the original wording.

Portland Brewer and I recently saw one where the letters were so scrambled that it looked as if the sign was speaking in tongues.

In front of a Pentecostal church.

True story.

When I got to the King homeplace, I turned in at the long sweeping driveway that led up to the house past newly planted baby azalea bushes that would someday grow into head-high masses of pink and white.

Aunt Zell's irises had been spectacular at Easter—like stalks of white orchids, six or seven blossoms to the stalk—but they needed dividing again and she'd already given some to every gardener she could think of. Then she remembered that Mrs. Avery's mother used to have white irises growing in her dooryard, "so I called Grace King Avery and she was thrilled because her brother didn't care anything about the gardens. Just let them go. I said I'd send her some divisions at first passing and as long as you're going right by her door . . ."

As I drove around to the back (no matter how splendid the front door on a country dwelling, few people use it), I was glad that I'd opted for a new house instead of going Grace King Avery's route. There's nothing more beautiful than a gracious old farmhouse lovingly restored, but they're black holes when it comes to time and money. I hate to think how many gallons of paint it took to cover all the turned railings and gingerbread on the front and side porches alone.

Raymond Bagwell was hard at it with a shovel when I

rolled to a stop. Stripped to his skinny waist, he was digging up a four-by-twenty length of sunbaked dirt that was probably going to be Mrs. Avery's restored perennial border.

"Raymond, right?" I asked as I got out of the car.

"Yes, ma'am," he said warily.

"I'm A.K.'s aunt."

"The judge?" He paused in his digging and gave my ball cap a skeptical look.

"That's me. Mrs. Avery here?"

He nodded toward the screen door and got on with his shovel.

A medium-sized white dog came over to greet me. Halfway between a spitz and a sheepdog, with a thumbprint of black hairs on the top of his head, he sniffed at my legs as I unlocked the trunk and lifted out the cardboard carton of iris tubers. Before I could slam the trunk lid, Grace King Avery was there, welcoming me, scolding Raymond for not helping me with the bulky box—"Just set it over there in the shade. And if you could just give them a sprinkle with the hose so they don't get too dried out? Zell did just dig them today, didn't she, Deborah? Not too much there, Raymond! I said sprinkle, not soak. Come in, Deborah, I was just thinking about you."

Useless to say that I was in a hurry. She and the dog were already leading me through the kitchen—"You wouldn't believe the way my brother let this place go. I had to buy all new appliances"—and into a large and airy room lined with floor-to-ceiling bookcases between the tall casement windows. All the woodwork sported a fresh coat of white enamel.

"This is where my father and my grandfather, too, did their accounts," she said. "That desk has sat in that very spot for over a hundred years."

The desk was solid and pleasingly crafted but probably built right here in the neighborhood by some nineteenth-century cabinetmaker who was good with his hands. It was not a piece to drive an antique dealer wild with envy unless he could see it with Mrs. Avery's ancestor-addled eyes, but it did look at home here. The dog curled up in the kneewell and went to sleep.

"My grandmother had her sewing machine over there in the corner," she said, nodding toward the spot where a large television now sat, "but I'm going to use this room as my den *cum* library."

(Mrs. Avery's probably the only person in Colleton County who could use the word *cum* and not sound pretentious.)

I'd never been inside this house before and I was surprised by its charm. There was an ease to the proportions that made you feel as if you could take a deep breath in comfort here, so I praised the desk and the room even though it was still cluttered with boxes of books and papers waiting to be arranged on the newly painted shelves as soon as they were completely dry.

Looking more than ever like a little gray-feathered guinea hen, Mrs. Avery picked her way through the maze of cardboard boxes and plucked a paper from one of them. "I came across this last night while I was looking for something else. Do you remember it?"

It was a creased sheet of lined paper that had been torn from a spiral-bound notebook and folded into a tight little packet. On one side, *Pass to Portland*. On the other side, *Ask Howard if he wants to take me to K.'s party, okay? D.*

The pencilled handwriting was my affected teenage loops and swirls right down to the little smiley face over the i. I felt my cheeks flame with the same embarrassment as when she'd confiscated that note in her classroom a hundred years ago.

Mrs. Avery shook her head at me. "Oh, you were a one all right. Always thinking about the boys. And now here you are a judge and still unmarried. I thought surely—"

"Time has a way of playing tricks," I said hastily. I crumpled the note, stuck it in my pocket and fished a high school yearbook from the nearest carton. It was from a few years back when one of my brother Robert's daughters was a freshman. It would be hard to open any one of these yearbooks and not see a Knott face somewhere in its pages.

"Blessed if I know why I haven't thrown out all these old test papers and record books," Mrs. Avery said. "Really, the yearbooks should be souvenirs enough, don't you think? Thirty-five years."

I was appalled. Thirty-five years of pounding sophomore English into the thick skulls of hormonal teenagers?

"No wonder you're enjoying this change of pace," I said.

"I've never worked so hard, but it's such pleasure," she

agreed. "The front parlor and bedrooms are still to do over, but they'll have to wait until I've finished up outside. After all those years in town, it's so wonderful to be out here on King land where everything I see is beautiful and orderly. Come and let me show you what I've done with my mother's roses. They're the only thing my brother cared about. Isn't it funny how men are with roses?"

I would soon have to be thinking about landscaping the grounds around my own house, so I was actually interested as she pointed out rhododendrons and camellias and how the gardenias needed good air circulation so they wouldn't mildew and if I wanted some of the baby magnolias that had volunteered around the mother tree, I should say now before she had Raymond root them out.

She had planted more azaleas on the slope down to the narrow creek branch that ran between her property and the little dilapidated church just on the other side. Here in the heat of summer, the branch was barely a trickle of clear water.

"A water garden with papyrus and blue flags would be so pretty down there, but—Come back here, Smudge!" she called sharply before her dog could cross the branch and muddy his paws. "My grandfather, Langston King, gave the land for that church, you know, so I can't help feeling an interest in it. I've offered to have Raymond mow their grass and neaten up a little, maybe haul off those old cars, but I'm afraid Mrs. Williams took my offer wrong."

She would, I thought, suppressing a grin. Women like

Grace King Avery could get me to agree to anything just to get rid of them, but Sister Williams was an implacable will that bent to no force.

Burning Heart of God Holiness Tabernacle, pastored by the hot-tempered Reverend Byantha Williams, hasn't had a fresh lick of paint in all the years I've known it and the tin roof sags precariously. The only thing that seems to hold up the branch side of the church is the ancient rusty house trailer backed up against that wall where Sister Williams lives with her four malevolent cats.

Out back, behind the tiny graveyard, two wrecked cars and what looked like an old washing machine or refrigerator were half covered by kudzu vines. Even junk can look picturesque when smothered in vines. Too bad that kudzu hadn't reached the church yet.

Maidie shakes her head over the condition of this church because the congregation is too poor and too small to do more than patch and mend. It's a dying church. Sister Williams's standards are too rigidly puritanical and most of the young people deserted to other churches years ago. The average age is something like sixty-five. But what the members lack in youth and money they make up in fervor, and the rickety walls really rock when Sister Williams starts preaching. She's in her seventies now and vows she'll keep the church going as long as two or three be gathered together there in His name.

We wandered back up to the house and I was framing a graceful goodbye when Mrs. Avery said, "Well, I'm sorry to rush you, Deborah, but you see how busy I am.

Do thank Zell for me. It was so kind of her to send the irises. Now, Raymond, before you leave, if you could just—"

Dismissed, I got in my car and eased back down the winding driveway, wondering if Raymond's parents were as worried about the upcoming weekend as Andrew and April were.

On the other hand, jail might just be the rest he needed after working for Mrs. Avery all week.

As I neared the farm, it occurred to me for the first time that I was going to have to give some serious thought to a new driveway. The long pond's on the back side of the farm and can be reached by several different tractor lanes which crisscross the land. My favorite runs across the Stancil farm, soon to be an upscale housing development complete with streetlights, sidewalks and golf course. Others are extensions of driveways belonging to Daddy and my brothers. If my family could monitor every time I came or went, to say nothing of every visitor's coming and going, I might as well stay at Aunt Zell's for all the privacy I'd be gaining.

Certainly there was no privacy today. As I cleared the woods and came up to the building site that looked out over the pond, I saw six pickups, a bright red sports Jeep, a white Toyota and two horses parked (or tied) out by the deck. I recognized three of the pickups as belonging to the work crew who hammered away on the inside. The rest had brought nieces and nephews and several of their friends who were diving off the end of my brand-new pier.

Farm ponds usually have such messy bottoms that wading out to swimming depth is enough to blight the fun of swimming because you know you're going to have to wade back in through all the muck. Two weeks earlier, a pile driver from Fuquay came and sank a double row of ten-inch creosoted poles out to where the water's ten feet deep. Then I had a lumber company deliver a stack of two-by-fours and pressure-treated boards and told A.K., Stevie, and the rest of the kids who still lived on the place that they could use the pier if they'd build it. I figured I might as well get a little work out of them since there was no way I'd be able to keep them off my half of the pond once the pier was built anyhow.

Before I could switch off the engine, Zach's daughter Emma was tugging at the door.

"Wait'll you try it!" she cried. Her hair was wet and so were her brown T-shirt and red shorts. "We just put the last nail in about an hour ago. You should've got here sooner. You could've been first off. This is so cool!"

Yeah!

Her excited voice took me back to when one of the promoters for a community pool tried to sign Seth and Minnie up for membership half my lifetime ago.

"It's going to be Olympic size with a wading pool for the little ones and water slides and high boards for the teenagers," the neighbor said. Being a brand-new teenager myself then, I was ready to run right home and beg Mother and Daddy to sign up as charter members, too.

No more yucky pond bottoms? No more skinned knees on those sharp creek rocks? No beating the banks and water first in case there were water moccasins around? No more squatting behind chigger-laden bushes if nature called?

Hot damn! Civilization was coming to Cotton Grove for sure.

Seth had looked around at the eager faces of his children and even though cash money was tight in those days, he was ready to pledge his financial support when the neighbor lowered his voice and added, " 'Course it'll be—*you* know—restricted?"

I'm told it's still restricted, but I don't have firsthand knowledge since none of us ever joined and no Knott ever swam there.

Uncle Ash and Aunt Zell have an in-ground lap pool for his heart and Robert and Doris have one of those big blue plastic prefab things out back of their house for their grandchildren, but unless we're at the coast, the rest of us have pretty much made do with Possum Creek.

This was going to be a lot more convenient and I wondered why some of my brothers hadn't done it a long time ago. Was it because the spring-fed ponds had been dredged for utilitarian reasons? For irrigation and fishing, not for swimming?

I walked out on the solid planking and admired everything the kids had done. As I stood on the very end, Herman's son Reese came up dripping from the water at my feet and grabbed my ankle. My ball cap flew off and I felt myself falling through the sunlit air to land with a huge splash in deep cool water.

Even with all my clothes on, it felt wonderful, although when I got my hands on Reese, I tried to sit on his head for catching me off guard like that.

Stevie, home on summer vacation from Carolina, was standing on the pier laughing his head off when Seth's Jessica gave him a mighty shove from behind.

Soon the water was swarming with fully clothed whooping and hollering kids, all from here in the neighborhood. Oh well, I thought. Kids—even farm kids—have so many sophisticated distractions these days. Maybe the pier's homespun novelty would wear off before my house was finished and this privacy thing became an issue. I missed A.K. and his sister, though. Normally they would be here with the rest.

When I was thoroughly cool, I climbed out and sat on the pier to squeeze water from my shirt and shorts.

"Hey, you know what?" said Emma, treading water in front of me. "For Deborah's housewarming gift, we ought to take up a collection and buy her a beach."

"A beach?" asked Stevie, who was floating nearby.

"Yeah. A dump truck full of sand. How much could it cost?"

"Do you know how many truckloads it'd take to make even a ten-foot-wide beach?" said her brother Lee. "It'd cost a pure fortune."

"And your only paternal aunt's not worth a fortune?" I cooed sweetly.

They all hooted and I had to scuttle down the planked pier toward land to keep from getting splashed again.

My sneakers squished with every step as I walked up to the house still dripping water. My ball cap was the only thing that had escaped a soaking.

Delight welled up in me as I viewed my new house. Pride of ownership, too. From the outside, it was starting to look like a proper dwelling now that the roof was on and most of the siding was up. The south windows had been set since I was last out, which meant that Sheetrocking couldn't be too far behind.

I had stopped at a store on the way out and filled a cooler with soft drinks and as I pulled it out of the trunk of my car, Will appeared at my elbow.

"Let me help you with that, little sister," he said, grabbing the other end.

Seth had offered to oversee the construction and Haywood was all set to get his feelings hurt if I didn't choose him even though both brothers were knee-deep in tobacco when the bank finished approving my loan and I was ready to break ground. Fortunately, summer is the slowest season in Will's auctioneering business and for some reason, he really wanted to do this for me. Since Will actually worked in construction for a couple of years after he left the farm, I agreed.

Will's my mother's oldest child, good-looking and a bit of a rounder. You can't always count on him to finish what he starts, but when he does work, he works smart. Sometimes the other boys feel a little jealous and say I'm more partial to Seth, so it helps when I can favor one of them over Seth.

We carried the cooler onto what would be a screened porch overlooking the pond and the others inside took a break and came out to join us for a cold drink and something from the snack bag I'd also brought.

They were a pick-up crew from here in the neighborhood—two white men, a Mexican, and a black man who was the only one who'd actually worked with steel framing before. According to Will, they'd each grumbled about it though. He hadn't been all that thrilled at working with the stuff himself. Yeah, yeah, he knew it was the wave of the future, termite proof, cheaper, more energy efficient, et cetera, et cetera.

"All the same, wood's more forgiving," he said every time the metal frames popped their bolts or threatened to wobble out from under the men.

Now that everything was braced six ways to Sunday, the house felt as sturdy to him as Adam's literature had promised.

"It might actually stand up in an earthquake," he teased me.

Earthquakes aren't a real big problem in North Carolina. I was more interested in hearing that the house could withstand the wind force of a hurricane and the jaws of industrial-strength termites.

As the men finished their break, Herman's Annie Sue came out on the porch. She wore a sleeveless yellow tee, cutoffs, and heavy leather work shoes with bright yellow socks. Her chestnut hair was tied back in a ponytail.

"I'm all caught up with you, Uncle Will," she said, un-buckling the tool belt from her sturdy waist. "Nothing more I can do till the Sheetrock's up. Hey, Deborah. One of those drinks got my name on it?"

"And a Nab," I said, holding out the bag.

She broke open the cellophane wrapper and bit into the cheddar crackers smeared with peanut butter. Orange crumbs showered down the front of her shirt.

Herman started teaching Reese about electricity before Annie Sue was born, but she's a better electrician than he'll ever be.

Will went back inside and the two of us sat there on the porch steps sipping our Diet Pepsis as we looked out over the long pond where her cousins and older brother still frolicked in the water at the end of the pier.

"Come on in," they cried, but we both shook our heads even though I was still damp from the water and Annie Sue was equally damp from her hot sweaty work.

Reese's truck radio was set on a golden oldies country station and scraps of tinny banjo and guitar music floated up to us. The sun baked us dry as it started its long slow slide down the western sky. A male bluebird swooped down on a grasshopper and flew off toward the woods. A field of shoulder-high corn rippled greenly at the edge of my new boundaries. Music, laughter and splashing on one side, the sound of hammers on the other, yet I could feel peacefulness sinking into my bones.

"You picked you one of the prettiest places on the whole farm," Annie Sue said, unconsciously echoing my own thoughts. "Least it *would* be one of the prettiest if you could get Uncle Haywood to take away that old greenhouse."

"He says he's going to refurbish it," I said.

"And you believe him?" she asked cynically.

Haywood gets enthusiasms but he and Will are a lot alike about sticking to things. The difference is that Will works smart while Haywood can only work hard.

About five years ago, Haywood decided he was going to get into truck farming in a big way. Cut back on tobacco, go heavy on produce.

"The man who gets the first tomatoes to market gets to the bank first, too," he said. "First truckload of watermelons you'n get five dollars apiece. Last load, you can't give 'em away for fifty cents."

So he bought some big metal hoops, covered them in heavy plastic sheets and built himself a greenhouse sixty feet long and twelve feet wide down at the far end of the pond where his and Andrew's land comes together. And he diligently sowed flats of tomatoes and watermelons. And when they were the right size, he transplanted them out into the fields where they promptly drowned in one of the wettest springs we'd had in years.

Undaunted, he tried again the second year and did indeed get the first truckload of local tomatoes to the market where they had to compete against the tomatoes and watermelons being trucked up from Georgia and South Carolina.

According to Seth, who keeps all the boys' farm records on his computer, Haywood netted about eighty-five cents on the dollar that year.

"I tried to tell him to grow yuppie things for the Chapel Hill crowd," Seth said. "Leeks, snow peas, or fancy peppers. But all he knows are tomatoes and watermelons."

That winter, a storm shredded the plastic walls and Haywood lost interest in his greenhouse. Yet there it still stands—overgrown with weeds, rusting away, tattered banners of plastic fluttering like fallen flags in every breeze, a blight on the landscape at the end of the pond, right smack-dab in the middle of my view.

"I could string it with Christmas tree lights," Annie Sue offered. "Turn it into found art?"

"I think that only works for urban areas," I said.

As we contemplated Haywood's eyesore, A.K. drove down the lane and pulled up at the edge of the pond. The kids fell silent as he got out and walked towards them and I could tell from their body language that they felt awkward.

From beside me, Annie Sue murmured, "Ruth's been crying all afternoon. Emma tried to get her to come over and help with the pier, but she wouldn't. God! A.K.'s such a jerk!"

But the worry in her voice betrayed her.

He must have been working on the pier either last night or early this morning because he scooped up a tool belt and one of the hammers that were piled on the bank.

"They say it might rain tomorrow," he said, tossing them into the cab.

The cousins came up to him then while their friends hung back, exchanging uneasy glances.

Suddenly, from Reese's truck came the raucous tones

of Elvis Presley's "Jailhouse Rock." Stricken, Emma
raced over to snap it off, turned the wrong knob and the
music blared louder than ever: "Everybody in the old
cellblock—"

Abrupt silence.

A.K. shrugged and gave a wry grin. "Good timing."

"Hey, man, we practiced," said Reese, trying to turn it
into a joke, knowing he'd done a couple of things just as
bad, knowing that there but for the grace of God . . .

"Yeah, well, see you guys."

As A.K. turned back to his truck, Annie Sue raced
down and gave him a hug. I followed and when I put my
arms around him, he clung to me for an instant as if he
were seven again instead of seventeen.

"You'll be all right," I whispered. "The jailer knows
who you are. Just go with the flow and you'll be fine,
okay?"

"Okay," he said shakily.

❧ 12 ❧

God already made my day.
—Goodwill Missionary Baptist

That evening, after the work crew had departed and
the kids had scattered to their Friday night diversions,
after I'd quit raking up pieces of shingles, scrap ends of
two-by-fours and bits of plastic pipes, I drove over to
visit with Daddy a few minutes and maybe get a bite to
eat.

But he and Cletus had eaten an early supper and gone
catfishing somewhere along Possum Creek, said Maidie.
She was there on the screened back porch, rocking in the
late afternoon shade and shelling butter beans for the
freezer. I pulled another rocking chair closer to the hull
bucket, fetched a pan from the kitchen and sat down to
help her.

"How come you never told me you know Cyl DeGraffenried?" I asked.

"Don't remember you ever asking," she said mildly as
her fingers rhythmically twisted the flat green pods and
nudged the beans loose with her thumb. "Besides, I can't

say as I *know* her. Except for Miz Mitchiner, she keeps herself *to* herself. Far as that goes, Miz Mitchiner, she ain't all that outgoing neither."

I ate a podful of tender raw beans. "Who's Mrs. Mitchiner?"

"Her granny. Lives out from Cotton Grove. Goes to Mount Olive."

"Any kin to that Horace Mitchiner that's a jailer at the courthouse?"

Maidie frowned in concentration and I could almost see pages of genealogical data scrolling past her eyes. She finally shook her head. "He might be a far cousin of her husband, but I *believe* he's from that bunch of Mitchiners on the other side of Dobbs and Mr. Robert Mitchiner was from right around here. 'Course, he's been dead almost forty years."

She poured her hulled beans into a large pot on the table, refilled her pan with more pods from the bucket that Cletus or Daddy had brought in from the garden, then settled back in her cane-bottomed rocking chair to shell and reminisce in earnest.

"Miz Mitchiner, she's had a hard life. Her brother's wife ran off and she had to raise his young'uns, too, 'cause he was right sickly and couldn't work much. And Mr. Robert, he got killed in a car wreck when their baby boy won't but two. Her onliest daughter Rachel was Cylvia's mother and Rachel—Lord, she was a sweet-tempered girl! Had the prettiest singing voice, to be sure. Used to sing lead in the choir. Anyhow, Rachel died of pneumonia when that little girl was just starting to school. All them children turned out good, though. Cylvia, too. But Miz Mitchiner's son Isaac, he got in some kind of trouble and he run off to Boston before he was full-growed and she ain't never heard another word from him in over twenty years. It has to grieve her."

"What sort of trouble?"

She shook her head. "Oh, honey. With all your brothers? And A.K.? And as long as you been a judge? You know what hotheaded young men are like."

"I mean, was it civil or criminal? Did he rob a place, maybe kill somebody?"

"I can't rightfully remember all the details," Maidie said, her forehead wrinkling as she tried. "But it won't nothing like that, though. It was more to do with fighting for our rights. Trying to get colored folks signed up to vote? But seems like I remember there was something about breaking some white boy's nose that might've meant going to jail? And later we heard there was a white girl that he'd messed with and her menfolks was after him. Anyhow, whatever it was, I reckon he figured it was time for him to get out of Dodge."

That was something my mother used to say all the time and it made me smile. I emptied a pod of beans into my mouth. They were crisp and tender and had an earthy sweetness of flavor. "So Mrs. Mitchiner raised Cyl here? I thought she came from down around New Bern."

"She does, she does. Her daddy found another light-skinned woman down there and that's the one raised her. But you know how it is with some women. I don't think she was mean or nothing, but she had girls of her own. Let's just say she didn't mind that Miz Mitchiner brought Cylvia up here every summer when she was little."

She threw another handful of hulls into the bucket that sat between us. "To do her daddy credit though, he promised Rachel before she died that he'd see she went on to school and he did and look how good she's done—district attorney! She always was brighter'n a silver dime."

"Cyl's that, all right," I agreed, trying to match her hull for hull. "But she sure is hard on young people that break the law. Especially young men."

Maidie nodded thoughtfully. "Probably because of her uncle running away like that. He made a lot over her and they say she took it awful hard when he left. He was only ten years or so older'n her and just as dark-complected as her—onliest one of Miz Mitchiner's family that was. All the others is real light."

(As someone smack-dab in the middle of the color chart, Maidie speaks of skin tones as casually as I talk about the color of someone's hair or eyes, but it does aggravate her if somebody preens herself on being light or puts another sister down for being too dark. "Like they was extra smart for deciding to get themselves born like that," she sniffs scornfully.)

"Best I recall, Cylvia must've been around eight or maybe nine the summer Isaac run off. They say she 'bout cried herself sick and after that, she didn't come as much or stay as long."

Was it that uncomplicated, I wondered, nibbling on

more raw beans. A girlchild so wounded by her young uncle's abrupt flight that she unconsciously tried to punish every young black male who strayed from the straight and narrow?

"You keep on eating my beans," Maidie said, "and they ain't gonna be none to freeze. You so hungry, why don't you go get you some of that ham I fixed for supper?"

"Ham?" I suddenly realized just how hungry I was. "Maybe I'll fix a sandwich to take with me," I said, abandoning the beans as abruptly as Isaac Mitchiner had abandoned his niece.

An hour later, I sat on the steps of my own house and watched the sun set redly over the tips of the tall pines half a mile away that mark the edge of Andrew and April's backyard. Shorter oaks, and maples, now in the full leaf of summer, ranged closer, flanked by a thicket of scrub pines, wild cherries, dogwoods and sassafras that bordered the broad fields of corn. A warm breeze blew from that direction and carried the smell of tasseling corn, the promise of dryer air tomorrow, the plaintive call of a mateless and lonely chuck-will's-widow.

You and me, bird, I thought, feeling vaguely sorry for myself as the red sky deepened to purple and a pair of bats flitted across the pond in jittery dives and abrupt zigzags to snatch invisible insects from the air.

On the concrete porch floor beside me, my cell phone lay silent. When he called this morning, Kidd had asked where I was going to be tonight and he sounded pleased when I said I'd probably work out here till dark and then I'd go take supper with one of the boys or visit Daddy for a while.

"How 'bout I call you there around seven-thirty?" He had helped me site the house and knew its surroundings quite well by now. "You be on your porch, I'll stand on my deck and we'll see the sun go down together, watch the same stars come out."

"And who says men aren't romantic?" I'd teased.

But the sun had already set, the moon was glowing brightly overhead and still he didn't call.

Despite my ham sandwich, my resolve was weakening on that last pack of Nabs in the paper bag and I was just reaching for it when the phone finally trilled.

"Hello?"

"Sorry I'm late." Kidd's voice was warm and choco- laty smooth in my ear, making me hungrier for him than for all the cheese crackers in the world. "Amber needed a ride to her friend's house out in the country and I couldn't get back in time. Are you still out at the pond?"

"Yes," I said. "Looking for Venus and wishing you were here to show me Mars."

He chuckled and I knew he was hearing the double meaning.

"Oh damn!" I murmured as headlights flashed through the trees that lined Possum Creek and jounced down the lane toward me.

"What?"

"Someone's coming. I don't believe this. I've been out

here by myself for over an hour and now that you've finally called—"

I tried to make out the shape of the vehicle—car or truck?—but the headlights were blinding.

"Let me get rid of them and I'll call you right back," I said as I rose to my feet and tried to squint past the brightness.

"No, wait," he said. "You're there alone. Find out who it is before you hang up."

"Good idea," I said.

A split second later, I was standing there stunned as Kidd turned off the headlights and stepped from his van with a big grin on his face and his phone in his hand.

"Surprised?"

The word came doubly, through the dusk and through the receiver at my ear, and for the next few minutes, all I could say between laughter and kisses was "You turkey!"

"Surprised?" he asked again, his forehead touching mine.

"Totally and utterly."

There was a waste of more valuable airtime before we finally remembered to turn off our phones.

Arm in arm, we walked around to the back of the van. He lifted the hatch and I saw that the space was stuffed with camping equipment: tent, sleeping bags, cookware, a cooler full of cold beers and a big chilled steak that made me hungry all over again.

We pitched the tent at the edge of the pond near the pier and I pumped up the air mattresses while Kidd started a fire. We had camped twice before, once in the mountains, once on the Outer Banks, so I knew the drill. Mostly, it was to keep out of his way while he laid out the gear as efficiently as Aunt Zell putting away groceries in her own kitchen.

A Tupperware bowl held tossed salad greens and there were crusty rolls, tin plates to put them on and real knives and forks to eat with. When the meat came off the grill, charred on the outside and atavistically rare on the inside, it was the most delicious steak I'd put in my mouth since the one he'd cooked at Blowing Rock.

I popped the tops on two Heinekens and we ate sitting on the pier with our bare feet dangling in the water.

Our plates were soon clean, but other hungers still raged as we turned to each other. The smell of him—his aftershave, his clean cotton shirt—the taste of his steak-smeared lips against mine, the heat of his hands that ignited all my senses as they slipped beneath my shirt and unhooked my bra.

He wasn't wearing a belt and when I undid the buttons, his jeans slipped easily from his slim hips.

The planks on the deck were still warm from the hot June sun and after all our appetites were finally sated, we lay on our backs looking up at the stars. The moon was halfway to full. It sequinned the pond as we slid into the water and glistened on our wet bodies as we twined around each other like silvery eels in the moonlight.

*   *   *

That night, we zipped our sleeping bags together to form a double mattress and we slept on top of them with only a light sheet for cover. The sun woke us a little after five and it seemed so natural for Kidd to be there beside me that I didn't care how awful I must look: tangled hair, fuzzy mouth, no makeup.

"You look beautiful," he said, pulling me down on him.

By the time Will and his crew arrived at seven, we'd already had breakfast, put the camp in order and were clearing the floors of debris so that Sheetrock could be delivered on Monday as scheduled.

Kidd is good with his hands (no double entendre intended) and under Will's supervision, we installed the doors for my two-car garage and built a workbench along one wall. I hadn't planned on a garage at all, but Will talked me into it.

"Open carports let the whole world know at a glance if you're home or not, or whether you've got company," he'd said with the sly smile of one who'd slipped his car into someone else's garage a time or two. "Besides, you'll be glad for the extra storage space."

Now, as Kidd and I built shelves over the workbench, I could appreciate Will's reasoning. I would never own enough stuff to fill these shelves, but in months to come, it might cut down on my family's raised eyebrows if Kidd's van were discreetly stowed behind thick aluminum doors, so I hammered and sawed with a will despite the sweat trickling down my face.

At noon, Will paid the men their week's wages in cash and I wrote him a check that covered his time, too.

"Everybody keep their act together, you could be moving in by the end of July," Will said.

"It's looking real good," I told him, but he frowned as he gazed out past the pond to the dilapidated greenhouse.

"We sure do need to get Haywood to pull that ugly thing off. You speak to him about it?"

I nodded. "He says he's going to fix it up."

"I'd stick a match to it," Will said, "only there's nothing there to burn."

After he'd gone, Kidd and I drove over to Seth's and borrowed a couple of horses and spent the afternoon riding along back lanes, catching up on a week's worth of small talk. By the time we'd unsaddled the horses and turned them back out to pasture, I was feeling truly gamey and sat on the far side of the van's front seat as we drove in to Dobbs.

"Kidd! How nice," said Aunt Zell as she opened the screen door for us. "Y'all are just in time for drinks."

The back porch was deep and shaded. It ran the full width of the house and was a cool place to sit on a hot afternoon. The beds of bright flowers just beyond the screen echoed the crisp floral chintz on Aunt Zell's new patio cushions. A bowl of peanuts and a plate of raw vegetables sat on the glass-topped table.

Uncle Ash set his glass down and walked over to the door of his den. "Bourbon for you, son, or gin-tonic? Unless you'd like to shower first, too?"

I left Kidd in their capable hands and went upstairs.

My rooms on the second floor had begun as an apartment for Uncle Ash's elderly mother years ago. Although connected to the main house, it had its own separate entrance and had been a convenient place to perch while trying to figure out what I was doing with my life. I could even feel virtuous about staying on after I was earning enough to get my own place because Uncle Ash's job as a tobacco buyer meant lots of travelling both here in the States and in South America and he didn't like to leave Aunt Zell alone. But now that he would be retiring at the end of the summer, the time was more than right for me to move out.

Nevertheless, I was starting to feel nostalgic already as I moved through the cool, pale green rooms, undressing while I went till I stepped naked into the shower.

I lathered with scented soap and shampoo and decided that hot water on tap has to be one of civilization's greatest luxuries.

"Unless it's air-conditioning," said the pragmatist in my head as I towelled off and let the cool air flow over me.

"Amen," agreed the preacher.

I dried my hair, twisted it up in a loose knot which I secured with a couple of enameled clips, slid on a sleeveless blue dress that matched my eyes and put on a pair of dancing shoes in case we dropped by one of the clubs in Raleigh. Lipstick, mascara, and I was ready to ride.

During the week, I try to act mature and judge-like.

❖ 13 ❖

*Less confrontation
More communication
—Freedom Chapel*

Maidie had promised to save us seats if we got to Mount Olive early enough and a young girl, dressed all in white right down to the small white beads braided into her hair, was on the watch for Aunt Zell, Uncle Ash and me as we walked up the gravel drive from the parking area beside the church. She looked about twelve or thirteen, that endearing time when they teeter between childhood and adolescence, more at ease in sneakers than the one-inch heels she wore this morning.

As she handed us program leaflets, the tilt of her head, her deep-set eyes and something about her shy smile made me ask, "Aren't you kin to Jimmy White?"

"Yes, ma'am," she said. "He's my momma's daddy."

"You're Alice's daughter?"

"Wanda's," she murmured and led us inside and down the aisle to where Maidie was seated.

Alice had been a year ahead of me in school, Wanda

two years behind. Sometimes I feel as if I'm the only graduate of West Colleton High who hasn't gone forth, been fruitful and multiplied.

Mount Olive's interior was as classically simple as its exterior. Sunlight streamed through the frosted glass windows into a large open space of dazzling brightness. Aunt Zell, Uncle Ash and I walked down an aisle carpeted in a royal blue that matched the pew cushions. Painted on the wall behind the choir was a large colorful mural of John the Baptist standing on the bank of the river Jordan with Jesus, ready to baptize him. Everything else was painted white: walls, ceilings, all the trimwork. Even the sturdy plantation-made pews had a hundred and fifty years' worth of white enamel on them.

Four big white wooden chairs, seats and backs padded in royal blue leather, stood between the simple hand-carved pulpit and the choir stall like ecclesiastical thrones. I recognized the Reverend Anthony Ligon, who pastored here, and the activist attorney Wallace Adderly, of course. Sitting between Adderly and Ligon was the Reverend Floyd Putnam, a white preacher from Jones Chapel Baptist Church in Cotton Grove. On the other side of Adderly was the Reverend Ralph Freeman.

Sunday School wasn't over yet and already the sanctuary was three-fourths full as Uncle Ash let me slide in beside Maidie. I glanced around and found more white faces than one usually saw at these things. I expected there would be even more for the picnic lunch. Mrs.

Avery sat next to Jack and Judy Cater from Sweetwater and my friends Portland and Avery Brewer were there from First Baptist in Dobbs along with Chief District Court Judge Ned O'Donnell. Luther Parker nodded gravely from the end of the pew across from us and Louise gave me a wink.

To my surprise, I realized that the person in front of them with her eyes firmly fixed on the wall painting was Cyl DeGraffenried.

"An upright young black woman in a black church— why should that surprise you?" asked the preacher from deep inside my skull.

"Upright but uptight. Maybe a political move?" wondered the pragmatist.

Now that I thought about it, I couldn't tell if it was the imminent baptism of Jesus that held her attention or one of the men on the left. Wallace Adderly or Ralph Freeman.

The church was filled with the hum and murmur of voices as we waited for Sunday School to be over at eleven. Even the preachers and Wallace Adderly were talking together in low rumbles. I leaned my lips to Maidie's ear and whispered, "Is Cyl DeGraffenried a member here?"

"Never moved her membership up from New Bern," Maidie whispered back, "but here's where she was baptized. That's her granny sitting next to her. Miz Shirley Mitchiner."

Just then, a large woman in a blue lace dress and wide-brimmed white hat came in from a side door, went to the piano, and without hesitation swung straight into a rollicking hymn. Children and adults streamed in from the Sunday School classrooms. They filled the few remaining empty pew spaces and soon lined all the sides.

Singing a joyful praise song, the choir marched down the aisle in royal blue robes with white satin collars and took their places in the stall behind the pulpit.

The director signalled and soon we were all standing and singing and clapping in time to "He's Got the Whole World in His Hands."

My mind often wanders during the sermon and today was no exception after Reverend Ligon introduced "my brother in Christ, the Reverend Floyd Putnam from Jones Chapel right here in Cotton Grove."

Putnam was an earnest droner and even though the congregation encouraged his peace-and-harmony platitudes with polite amens and murmured yeses, he never caught fire and I soon found my thoughts drifting to Cyl and her grandmother.

From where I sat, I could see both profiles. Mrs. Mitchiner was at least seventy. She wore a rose linen suit, and a smart hat of pink roses covered most of her white hair. Her skin was so pale that she could probably pass for white if she chose, while Cyl was a dark rich brown. Mrs. Mitchiner's nose was aquiline and her mouth had a thin-lipped severity. Cyl's nose was slightly broader, her lips much fuller. If there was a family likeness, it wasn't in facial features. Rather, it was the way they both sat so erectly, almost stiffly, their backs barely touching the back of their pew.

I wondered what it must have been like to grow up the darkest member of a light-skinned family. Had her step-mother made her feel like Cinderella? Had her fairer half-siblings and cousins taunted her? Colleton County must have seemed doubly lonely after her uncle left, which made me wonder all over again why she was still here. Her grandmother?

And why had she been crying in my office on Thursday? This wasn't the first time I'd cast my mind back to that morning, but I could think of nothing in the usual lineup of minor offenses she had prosecuted that should've brought tears. Besides, she'd been distracted from the minute court began. Maybe something happened before she came to work? It occurred to me again that I didn't have the slightest notion of Cyl DeGraffen-ried's private life. For all I knew, she could have a live-in lover and six kids.

Well, okay, maybe not kids. Someone would have noticed if she had kids; but if she had a private lovelife . . .

Which brought my thoughts around to Kidd again. By now he was probably stopping in Goldsboro for a barbe-cue sandwich on his way back to New Bern and God alone knew when our schedules would next mesh.

The Reverend Floyd Putnam called for prayer and I automatically bowed my head and closed my eyes, but I'm afraid my prayers were more temporal than spiritual.

"Amen!" said Mr. Ligon when Mr. Putnam's tepid prayer drew to a close. "You've given us a lot to think about this morning, Brother Floyd, and we thank you. But before we go any further, we want to welcome

Brother Ralph Freeman and the whole congregation of
Balm of Gilead here today. As most of you know, Balm
of Gilead burned down Wednesday night. The Bible tells
us to curse the deed, not the doer and we give thanks to
our Lord Jesus Christ that no one was hurt."

("Yes, Lord!" came the murmurs. "Praise Jesus!")

"Brother Ralph's family is with him here today and
I'm asking them now to stand up and be known to you.
Sister Clara? Stan? Lashanda?"

An attractive, slightly plump woman of early middle
age with processed hair stood up in the front row and
smiled shyly as welcoming sounds washed over her from
the congregation. Her son Stan was probably thirteen or
fourteen and looked as embarrassed as most teenagers are
when the spotlight hits them, but his younger sister
beamed from ear to ear.

Another twenty or more people got to their feet when
Mr. Ligon called for the members of Balm of Gilead to
stand. I wondered which were the strayed sheep that Maidie was annoyed about but decided this wasn't the time to
ask her.

The choir sang again—"The Storm Is Over Now"—
and again we all joined in at the end. Then Wallace
Adderly was introduced and Mr. Ligon promised that
we'd get to hear him speak after lunch, but now we
should welcome the words of Brother Ralph Freeman.

Ralph Freeman was as dynamic as Floyd Putnam had
been dull. He, too, talked of trying to live in peace and
harmony and racial goodwill, but somehow his words

spoke to the heart and made the spirit sing. For that twenty minutes, he made us believe that Martin Luther King's dream really could happen, that people might quit letting their eyes stop at a person's skin but keep on looking deeper until each saw the other's humanity.

His face glowed, his words soared and we were caught up in it, longing to believe, aching for the communal unity that bound us together for this brief moment.

After Mr. Freeman concluded, Reverend Ligon poured benedictions down upon us and then the choir led us out into the sunshine of a perfect Sunday morning in the South.

Back when I was a very little girl, dinner on the grounds was just that: a picnic dinner spread on long tables beneath tall oaks or pecan trees, with wooden tubs of lemonade and iced tea at either end and every food known to the congregation's women in between.

Yes, yes, I *know* it's probably healthier to eat inside in air-conditioned coolness, away from the heat and flies and the dust kicked up by unruly children playing tag around the trees. And certainly it's more comfortable to sit at a table rather than trying to balance paper plates and cups while standing up outside. Nevertheless, dinner on the grounds loses some of its picnic charm when serving tables are set up in a fellowship hall and people sit in folding chairs at long rows of tables draped in white paper tablecloths rather than walking around to mingle with this one, exchange compliments and recipes with that one, before finding a place to perch with yet another.

Uncle Ash and I fetched the cooler from the car and Aunt Zell set out her fried chicken, potato salad and watermelon pickles next to Maidie's chicken pastry and huge bowl of butter beans while the men stood around outside, smoked, talked about the fire, and waited to be called in to eat.

With so many picnic boxes and coolers already stowed under the table, there was no more room for Aunt Zell's and I slipped out a side door to carry it back to the car. As I rounded a clump of boxwood shrubs, I almost bumped into a skinny black man of indeterminate middle age.

Clouds of alcoholic fumes enveloped me and I registered his soiled white shirt half tucked into his pants and a wrinkled tie that hung limply over the collar, its knot halfway down his thin chest.

"Lemme help you with that," he said, grabbing woozily for the bulky cooler.

"That's okay," I said, trying to sidestep.

"Naw, I'm 'sposed to *help*," he insisted.

Before it could turn into a full-fledged tug of war, Mr. Ligon suddenly appeared.

"Arthur!" he said sternly and the man let go so abruptly, I would have fallen backwards if Mr. Ligon hadn't caught me.

"I apologize for our sexton's behavior, Judge." He glared at the other man, who seemed to shrink back into the bushes.

"That's okay," I said. "It was nice of him to offer to carry this, but it's really very light."

I swung the cooler by one handle to demonstrate, nodded pleasantly and kept on walking. Behind me, I could hear Mr. Ligon speaking with controlled fury, then the sound of a door closing.

I looked back. They were nowhere in sight. I took a closer look and realized that the boxwoods screened a door that I hadn't noticed till then. It was covered in the same white clapboard as the fellowship hall and the break was barely visible.

When I returned from stowing the cooler in the trunk of Uncle Ash's Lincoln, the door was half open. I could hear the drunken man rage, "You can't kick me out. I'll tell the deacons. I'll tell 'em all about you!"

"Tell whatever you want," said the Reverend Ligon in an equally angry voice, "but come next week, your sorry behind is out of here!"

I scooted past the boxwood bushes and was well inside the fellowship hall when Mr. Ligon came through to inquire genially if it was nearly time to ask the blessing.

By one-thirty, I was as stuffed as one of Maidie's deviled eggs. Across the table from me, Judy Cater, who's the reference librarian at the Colleton County Library in Dobbs, tried to give me a piece of her pecan pie.

"No way," I said.

"But this one's made without corn syrup so it's not too sweet," she coaxed.

I am always tempted by pecan pie no matter what the

recipe, but what's the good of church if it can't stiffen your resolve to resist temptation in all its many forms?

As the last sips of iced tea were slipping down our collective throats, the Reverend Ligon stepped up to the speaker's podium at the end of the hall and called us to order. He made a graceful thank-you speech for all the delicious food, praised God for the fellowship, then announced that he wanted to recognize all the dignitaries who turned out today to make this interchurch meeting such a success.

Indeed, there were a lot more whites than one usually sees at something organized by black Christians. But after Balm of Gilead's burning Wednesday night, I guess the mostly white establishment wanted to avoid the risk of being thought insensitive. All but two of the county commissioners were here, the Clerk of Court, the superintendent of public schools, Sheriff Bo Poole, DA Doug Woodall and "our own Miss Cylvia DeGraffenried," the county manager, and of course, Ned O'Donnell, Luther Parker and me.

The list went on: the president of the Democratic Women, a tall and stately black woman; her Republican counterpart, equally tall, equally stately, white; even Grace King Avery was recognized as returning to "her roots, to her homeplace here in the community after years of educating our young people on the importance of good English."

It was almost two o'clock before he turned the microphone over to Wallace Adderly.

Adderly was savvy enough to know that after a heavy meal and long introductions, somnolence was ready to take over his audience. Impulsively, he called to the choir director and soon the whole hall was rocking with an a cappella version of "This Little Soul Shines On."

If the Reverend Freeman was the conciliatory side of Martin Luther King, Wallace Adderly was his militant. Settling his gaze on one white official after the other, he exhorted us to take this morning's spirit of fellowship back into our neighborhoods, our workplaces and (fixing his eyes on me) our courtrooms; to put our principles into economic and social practice.

To his fellow blacks, he sounded a clarion call to face up to new responsibilities and renewed challenges, to quit whining about the past and to accept that there never had been and never would be any free lunches in America. "What's passed for free lunches—namely, welfare—has merely been another way to keep the poor and uneducated in a state of dependency. It's time we all start paying the full price for what we believe we deserve."

It seemed to me that he was pretty much preaching the substance of Cyl DeGraffenried's text and my eyes searched the crowd for her face. I finally located her two tables over, but to my surprise, she wasn't sitting in Adderly's amen corner. Indeed, her chair was pushed so far back from the table—and Wallace Adderly—that she crowded the person behind her. She sat rigidly with her arms locked tightly across her chest and her lovely face was frozen into an expression of intense loathing.

❧ 14 ❧

A hint is something we often drop
But rarely pick up
*   —Friendly Chapel Pentecostal*
*   Free Will Baptist*

Word of the fires spread through the county, to the state, and leapfrogged Washington to New York.

During the night, news teams from all up and down the eastern seaboard swarmed through the Triangle. Microphones were stuck in the faces of everybody who answered a knock at the door or stood frozen in the camera lenses. Somebody thought they spotted Cokie Roberts in Raleigh that morning and another swore that Peter Jennings had been seen ducking into the ABC affiliate on Western Boulevard.

Cotton Grove itself, indeed the whole western part of Colleton County, seemed to be in shock, but everyone—everyone except the Reverend Byantha Williams perhaps—said it was a blessing that the arsonist had begun with Mount Olive. If Burning Heart of God had been torched first, the volunteer fire trucks would have been out there, trying to save that tumbledown excuse for a church while one of the most historically significant buildings in the county burned to the ground.

Instead, it was Sister Williams who was completely homeless and churchless when the sun came up red-hot on Monday morning.

"Praise God for Sister Avery here," said the elderly preacher as television cameras zoomed in on the black hand that clasped the white hand of her rescuer. A hostile tabby cat sat in her lap and hissed at the interviewer. "She took me in and she saved my life."

"Not I," Grace King Avery said quickly, patting Sister Williams's hand. "Smudge deserves all the credit. He was so restless last evening that he made me nervous."

She smiled down at the dog that sat quietly on its haunches beside her, well away from the cat's claws. Except for that dark patch of gray hairs between its ears, it was all white, and its black eyes gleamed with intelligence whenever she spoke.

"I'd already locked up for the night." Mrs. Avery wore a fresh, pale blue shirtwaist and her gray hair was neat and tidy in its usual bun, but the lines in her face and her red-rimmed, puffy eyes attested to a stressful night without sleep.

"Smudge just wouldn't settle down. He kept acting as if somebody were prowling around down by the barn, so I turned on all the outside lights and that's when I heard a car start up across the branch and drive away. A minute later, the whole back of the church seemed to go up in flames. It was just sheer luck that I was watching."

"Not luck, honey," insisted the Reverend Williams, who looked larger than life-size in a capacious cotton robe splashed with bright red and orange flowers. "God was directing your eye last night. His eye is on the sparrow and He put your eye on me."

Once again she launched into the story of how she'd gone to bed at nine-thirty last night and was already sound asleep when she heard Mrs. Avery banging on the door of her little trailer. "She was yelling Fire, Fire! and said I had to get out. Well, I couldn't find Puffcake and—"

We had already seen Channel 17's interview with these two women and heard Sister Williams's tale of rounding up her various cats, so Uncle Ash set down his coffee cup and flipped to Channel 11 where Miriam Thomas in the studio was adding a question of her own to the remote interview with my ATF friend Ed Gardner and the resident FBI agent who'd hastily flown over from Charlotte. More racial epithets had been found on one of Mount Olive's unburned walls.

"—so yes, Miriam, although it's much too early to say with complete certainty, our preliminary investigations show enough similarities to make us think that these two fires may indeed be linked to Wednesday night's burning."

Miriam Thomas and her partner, Larry Stogner, reminded viewers that Wednesday night was when Balm of Gilead burned.

Every local news channel alternated between the smoldering remains of the two churches. At Burning

Heart of God, the only visible signs left behind the yellow police cordon were sheets of twisted tin from the roof and the burned-out hulk of Sister Williams's metal mobile home.

The cameras caught the fire chief shaking his head woefully.

"We're just too short of equipment," he said. "Way this part of the county's growing, we need at least a substation and another truck."

Standing behind him, Donny Turner nodded his head in strong agreement.

At Mount Olive, the damage looked awful, but much had been spared. The whole north end of the church was black and charred where only yesterday had been bright Sunday School classrooms, a robing room and the choir stall itself. Flames had destroyed the mural of Jesus with John the Baptist and had licked up against the ecclesiastical chairs before they were brought under control, but the fellowship hall next to the church looked like a total write-off. The fire had started there before jumping to the main building. The roof still stood, and so did an exterior wall with its crudely printed words in green spray paint—"Niggers back to Africa"—but the whole interior was a slurry of waterlogged charcoal.

"This is bad," said Aunt Zell, who was too distracted to fix anything more complicated than toast for our breakfast. "This is really just too bad."

Uncle Ash shook his head as he pulled a burned slice from the toaster and handed it to me.

I put it on the plate in front of me and tried again to

call Andrew and April, but once again the operator came on the line: "We're sorry. All our circuits are currently busy. Please hang up and try your call again later."

It was the same when I tried Seth's number, Daddy's and Haywood's. Nothing was getting through to their exchange.

I left the toast on my plate and headed for Cotton Grove. If I didn't get caught behind any tractors, there was just enough time to make it there and back to Dobbs before court convened.

I may have pushed the speed limit a little as I drove west in the early morning sunlight. Traffic didn't seem much heavier than usual, but then I was zipping through back roads and shortcuts. I took the homemade bridge across Possum Creek so fast that for a minute I thought I'd busted one of my shocks.

When I pulled up to the back porch of Andrew's house, Dwight Bryant was standing by his departmental car there in the yard and Daddy was leaning against his pickup. A.K. and Andrew were on their tractors, ready to head out to the field as if nothing had happened, and April's smile was serene and unworried.

No one seemed surprised to see me.

"I figgered you'd be out here once you seen the phones was all tied up," Daddy said.

"We'll go on then, Dwight," Andrew said, giving me a wave before he cranked his tractor and trailed A.K. down past the barns. Time and tobacco wait for no man.

"Everything's okay, then?" I asked inanely.

April's smile widened. "If you'd gone to church last night, you'd have known."

"Huh?"

"New Deliverance opened their revival last night."

Enlightenment dawned. New Deliverance is the borderline charismatic church over in Black Creek with a borderline Ayatollah for a preacher. Not my favorite place to worship by a long shot. But that's where my brother Herman and his wife go—Nadine's one of those strait-laced Blalocks from Black Creek—and she's always badgering different ones of us to come fellowship with them. To keep family peace, we occasionally do.

"Andrew went and promised Nadine we'd come," April said with a wicked grin, "and we decided it wouldn't hurt for A.K. to sit through one of their preacher's hellfire and brimstone sermons either."

"Ain't that cruel and unusual punishment?" Daddy asked me with a wink.

"And guess who was sitting in the row behind A.K. till almost ten o'clock?" asked Dwight.

"Who?"

"My mother."

I hooted with laughter and relief.

Emily Bryant is one of my favorite people. She has bright orange hair and drives a purple TR—a real catbird. But she's also the highly effective principal of Zachary Taylor High School, and her word carries weight.

"What about the other two boys?" I asked. "Raymond Bagwell and Charles Starling?"

"We're looking into that," he said repressively.

Normally I would have badgered him for more details but right now it was enough to know that A.K. wasn't involved and that I could drive back to Dobbs with a lighter heart and, with a little luck, maybe even get to court on time.

Provided Dwight or a highway patrolman didn't follow me, of course.

Cotton Grove's a twenty-minute drive to the west of Dobbs if you follow the posted speed limits, and with most of Colleton County's law enforcement agencies buzzing around out there, directing traffic around the two churches, Dobbs itself was relatively calm when I got back.

There was much head shaking in the courthouse halls and everyone had a theory. One of the records clerks postulated that the fire had been set by skinheads on their way back to Fort Bragg. "You know how violent they are."

My nominal boss, Chief District Court Judge F. Roger Longmire, was sure it would turn out to be kids high on drugs.

"No, no," said attorney Ed Whitbread. "The first fire might have been done out of white racism, but what if these last two were copycats looking to stir up more excitement?"

"Or," said a white bailiff, and here his voice dropped almost to a whisper, "what if they was set by somebody to make it look like things are bad here for colored folks?"

"By *somebody*, you mean someone from the black community?" I asked.

He shrugged and hitched up his pants. "It happens. Besides, I hear they can't find the guy they had living over at Mount Olive to take care of the place. Maybe he really *did* take care of the place, you hear what I'm saying?"

We heard.

"On the other hand," said Roger as we walked down the hall to our respective courtrooms, "we both know weirder things have happened. Did you see that sexton yesterday? Pickled worse'n Peter's peppers. Louise Parker told me that Ligon was going to recommend that the deacons fire him. Maybe he did get mad and decide to get even."

All I could think about was that green spray paint and the fact that the fires began well after A.K. and his cohorts were released from jail at five o'clock yesterday afternoon.

And then there was Dwight's evasive answer to my question.

That's why I wasn't surprised when lunch time rolled around and a bailiff told me that Bagwell and Starling were on ice downstairs in Sheriff Bo Poole's office while Ed Gardner was hunting up a U.S. magistrate to sign an arrest warrant. The newly enacted Anti-Church Arson Act makes burning a church a federal offense now, so ATF had jurisdiction.

"They were drunk as skunks and got themselves thrown out of a shot house at eight-thirty last night, less than three miles from Mount Olive," the bailiff said. "And nobody saw them after that. They say they went straight to Starling's trailer and slept it off there, but it's down at the very end of the trailer park and our people canvassed the place. So far, none of the neighbors can put Starling's car there before ten o'clock."

"Same green paint they used in the Crocker family graveyard?" I asked.

"Same green, same lettering. Good thing your nephew wasn't hanging with 'em last night."

By the time Starling and Bagwell were actually bound over in a federal courtroom so jammed with reporters that all cameras were banished, the charges had escalated. Under the new and tougher laws, death as a result of deliberate arson was now a capital offense and they were being held in our local jailhouse without bail.

As Ed Gardner described it for me later, the investigation had started in earnest that afternoon after all the coals cooled off enough and everybody'd gathered at Mount Olive.

"It was a real team effort," Ed said, ticking the participants off on his finger.

In addition to Ed and an ATF Special Agent In Charge who'd helicoptered over from Charlotte with the resident FBI agent, there were about twenty other ATF agents (twenty-one if you counted four-legged accelerant-sniffing Special Agent Sparky), two SBI arson investigators, a handwriting expert from the SBI who would measure and photograph the new graffiti and compare the results with the Polaroids taken at the graveyard— "He was sure wishing your brother hadn't made those boys clean it up so fast"—a couple of detectives with arson experience from Sheriff Bo Poole's department and a couple of members of the local volunteer fire department.

"What about Buster Cavanaugh?" I asked. "Don't tell me our county fire marshall wasn't there?"

"Yeah, well, we sorta forgot to call him and his nose was bad out of joint when he caught up with us."

Patrol officers kept reporters and cameras back behind the lines, but they couldn't do much about the two news helicopters that circled overhead all day.

"Least they didn't fly into each other and crash down on our heads," Ed said dryly.

They began with a physical examination of the whole exterior, paying particular attention to the graffiti, then moved over to the most damaged area of the fellowship hall, trying not to disturb any evidence that might still be there.

"Ol' Sparky hit on accelerant right away. We took samples from the floor and wall areas. This time there was no attempt to make it look like an accident. No electrical wires in that area, no appliances with heating elements, and no fancy delay devices either. They just broke in somehow—maybe busted a window. Judging by the pour patterns, once they got inside, they started sloshing gasoline or kerosene around. Soaked the rug and the curtains and some wooden chairs that were there, then put a match to the curtains."

With all that wood, it hadn't taken long.

Mr. Ligon had told them of his disgruntled church mouse and how drunk he'd been the afternoon before. He was worried that if Arthur Hunt hadn't started the fire, maybe he'd perished in it? They had probed the area around his room with no success.

"We'd about decided he'd taken off, then one of my buddies hollered from inside the church."

Sometime in the past, well before 1900, a false floor had been installed so that the choir could sit on tiered risers behind the minister. When the wall burned, so did the chairs and the risers and the false floor.

They found Arthur Hunt where he had fallen through both floors to the dirt beneath the church.

Video cameras whirred with new energy and there was a frenzied buzz from all the electronic still cameras when the sexton's charred body was rolled out on a draped gurney to the ambulance and sent to the Medical Examiner over in Chapel Hill.

❧ 15 ❧

He that feeds the birds
Will not starve His babes
—Hico Baptist Church

July the Fourth came three days later.

Despite the fiasco of the pig-picking Daddy had thrown for me the first time I ran for judge, he saw no reason not to do it again, and invitations had been distributed by voice or mail in early June for a Fourth of July blowout.

The problem with a party this size is that it quickly assumes a juggernaut momentum of its own and you can't stop it on a dime.

For a dime either, as far as that goes.

Deposits had been paid on rental tents and tables, the pigs had been ordered, the cabbages and the hushpuppy mix bought, cartons of soft drinks, paper plates and plastic utensils were piled high in my new garage, along with a stack of borrowed pots for boiling corn on the cob and pails for icing down the drinks. Plastic tubs already held a half-dozen watermelons and waited for the ice water that would chill them properly. Cousins were flying in from Atlanta and Washington.

Black citizens were still roiled up and angrily denounced the climate that could produce a Bagwell and Starling. Wallace Adderly had been on every local television channel and most of the radio talk shows to voice their basic concerns as he saw them.

"Churches are our key institutions," he said. "Not the schools, not city hall, not the playing fields and gymnasiums. When you burn a church, you do more than destroy a building. You strike at the very heart of the African-American community. Every white person in this state ought to rise up in shame for what has happened in this one small area, this despicable attempt to undermine the strength of a people who will not be denied."

Nevertheless, with both culprits in jail, and with offers of help pouring in from all over, tensions were easing and most of the media had pulled back to New York and D.C.

I had conferred with Seth's wife, Minnie, about whether a big political celebration would seem frivolous so soon after the burnings in which a man died. (Minnie's my campaign adviser and can usually read the community's pulse.)

"Life keeps moving," she said philosophically. "Some people are always going to pick fault, but let's quick go ahead and invite all the preachers in the community. We'll need to cook some extra hams and shoulders and that means Seth'll have to round up another cooker." She was already drawing up a mental list of things to do. "We'll ditch the beer kegs, stick to soft drinks and lemonade, and if we remember that poor man in our prayers and sing the national anthem before we eat, we should be okay."

I gave her a hug. "Hypocrite."

"God bless America," she said wryly.

With the new pier such a success, my family thought it'd be more fun to have the pig-picking where people could go swimming if they wanted to. Stevie and Emma had volunteered to lifeguard and we hung old sheets across a couple of doorless rooms in my new house to act as changing rooms.

Haywood and Robert set up the cookers beneath a clump of oak trees that used to shelter holsteins from the burning sun back when this pond was newly dug, back when what's going to be my front yard was a pasture. Two long blue-and-white-striped tents—one for serving the food and drinks, one for eating—were erected and staked down by Wednesday afternoon and folding tables were hauled in and set up underneath the tents before dusk. When I finally crawled into my old bed at the homeplace sometime after midnight on the third, everything that could be done ahead of time was done.

"You mama always liked a good party," Daddy said happily when I kissed him good night.

As I lay there listening to the familiar creaks and groans of the old house settling down for the night, I could almost hear Mother's light voice floating up the stairwell: "Deborah! Where did you put those tablecloths? Kezzie? You'll have to send one of the boys to the store for more plastic cups. And better tell him to get another carton of paper napkins while he's there."

And Daddy's exasperated roar. "Just how the hell many people you expecting, Sue? You promised me it was gonna be a *little* get-together this time."

"Now, Kezzie," Mother would say, then she'd flit off to take care of another dozen details that would make the weekend run smoothly.

What Daddy could never remember was that her idea of a good party was one that started on, say, a Wednesday and didn't end till after breakfast on Monday. Cousins and friends still miss my mother's parties. There would be picking and singing, maybe even a little dancing, marathon card sessions, lots of food and drink, people shoehorned into every cranny of the house with babies and teenagers sleeping on pallets spread across the floor. And all that was before local friends and relatives arrived for the real party on Saturday.

Daddy always grumbled about having to wait on line to use the bathroom, or being eaten out of house and home, but Mother would just smile and keep moving, knowing that he'd be standing right there on the porch beside her come Monday morning, telling their guests, "I don't see why y'all got to run off so quick. Seems like you just got here."

The Fourth dawned hot and hazy and by the time Maidie and I drove out to the pond, we could smell the smoky succulence of roast pork as soon as we stepped out of the car. Robert and Haywood were seated out by the cookers where they could keep their eyes on the thermometers. They'd rigged a makeshift table from a couple of ice chests and were playing gin.

Robert knocked with two points and I took advantage of the next shuffle to lift the lid and fish out a Pepsi. "What time did y'all put the pigs on?"

"Around six," said Haywood, looking suspiciously at the ace of spades that Robert had just discarded.

There are still purists who insist that the only way to cook pig is on a homemade grill over hardwood coals, but I'm here to tell you, people, it don't taste too shabby over gas either. All up and down North Carolina roads, from early spring to late fall, you'll see what look like big black oil drums on wheels being towed behind cars and pickups.

Pig cookers.

What you do is start with a basic two-wheel steel trailer and a 250-gallon oval oil drum. Then you take an acetylene torch and cut the drum in half lengthwise through the short wall. Weld the bottom half to your trailer, add hinges and a handle to the top half and a heavy rack to the bottom half. Scrounge some burners from your local gas distributor. Punch a hole in the top for your heat gauge and another hole in the bottom so the fat can drip out into a metal bucket. Add a small tank of propane gas and you've got what it takes to start cooking.

Of course, you do need a little experience to know when to flip the pig—too soon and it won't cook all the

way through, too late and it'll fall apart when you lift
it—and you really ought to have a secret sauce recipe
you can brag about even though most of the braggarts
just add the same basic five ingredients to cider vinegar.
It all eats good to me, but Haywood and Robert still
argue over just how much red pepper's needed.

"Gin!" said Haywood. "Did I catch you with a fist full
of picture cards?"

I waited till Robert finished adding up the score, then
asked, "How much longer till you turn them?"

"Getting hungry, shug?" Robert set down his cards.
"That little ninety-pounder's been going right fast. Let's
take a look."

He got up and walked over to the nearest cooker, Haywood and I right behind him. When he lifted the lid, a
cloud of smoke escaped, carrying wonderful smells. The
pig had been split from head to tail and lay on the grill
skin side up, split side down.

Robert laid his hand on one of the hams and looked at
his brother. "What do you think?"

Haywood flattened the palm of his own huge hand
against the shoulder ham, held it there a moment and
said, "I'n sure feel the heat."

"Let's do 'er then."

By now Seth and Minnie were there as well as Maidie
and four or five of my nieces and nephews. A raised
cooker lid draws more kibitzers than a game of solitaire.

Using old dishtowels as potholders, four of the men
each grabbed a foot and at Robert's signal, they gave a
heave and gently flipped the pig over so that it was now

skin side down over the gas burners. Eager fingers reached in to pick off hot crispy slivers of the tenderloin, mine right along with them.

"Hey, now," Robert scolded.

He swished a clean dishmop through the sauce and used it to slather the meat with a generous hand before closing the lid, ignoring all the pleas for just one more little taste.

"Y'all can just wait till everybody's here," he said firmly, even though Maidie pointed out that he'd had his fingers in, too. He just grinned, licked his lips, then he and Haywood wiped their hands and resumed their card game, so Maidie and I went on up to the tents to spread red-white-and-blue tablecloths and unfold chairs.

Since we expected people to drift in and out most of the afternoon, we had only rented enough tables and chairs to seat a hundred at a time. The rest would find perching places on the grass or along the pier.

Under the food tent, Amy and Doris had iced down the soft drinks in big garbage pails that had been bought for this purpose last party, and now they were slicing lemons into the wooden tubs. Sugar and water would be added and then the mixture could be left to steep itself into refreshing lemonade.

Will arrived with two iron stakes and a sledgehammer. "Where you think we ought to do horseshoes?"

I looked around for a level spot away from traffic lanes between the tents and the house. Jess and Ruth had erected a volleyball net down near the pond. "How 'bout around on the other side of the pier?" I suggested.

Robert's grandson Bert and Haywood's granddaughter Kim scampered past carrying bocce balls.

"Play with us, Aunt Deborah?" asked four year-old Kim.

There were probably a zillion things that still needed doing, but hey, how long do great-nieces and -nephews stay four? Besides, the way we play bocce, whoever's closest wins a point even if the ball in question is thirty feet away, so our games aren't very long.

By the time they lost interest and went to help tie red, white and blue balloons to my porch railing, the younger guests were arriving. I watched Andrew's Ruth go shyly out to meet her first real boyfriend. Soon a volleyball game was organized and several kids were already in the water.

Now cars began to stream in, filling the old pasture.

The Reverend Freeman arrived with his teenage son and seven-year-old daughter.

"Stan and Lashanda, right?" I asked.

"Yes, ma'am," Lashanda grinned. Her hair was braided into a dozen or more pigtails and each was clipped by playful yellow barrettes so that it seemed as if she was wearing a headful of yellow violets to match her yellow T-shirt.

She looked so cute that I had to hug her.

"Hey, dibs on Stan!" called one of my nephews from the volleyball court. "We need a good spike. Get in here!"

Zach's Emma came by and gathered up Lashanda.

"Did you bring your bathing suit? Good! I'll show you where to change."

"This is awfully nice of you, Judge," said Ralph Freeman. His handclasp was firm, his smile warm and friendly.

"It's Deborah," I told him.

His smile widened. "Then I'm Ralph."

"Actually, it's good you could come with all that's been happening. Have you found a place to hold services yet?"

"Well, Mount Olive offered to let us use their sanctuary after their second service, but now they're scrambling, too. For the time being, our board of deacons has come up with an old-fashioned revival tent. We're going to pitch it on our new site."

"That's right. I heard that Balm of Gilead was selling its land to Shop-Mark, but I didn't know you were that close to groundbreaking on a new church."

Freeman gave a rueful laugh. "Talk about the Lord working in mysterious ways. We thought the land we wanted was out of our range, but when Balm of Gilead burned, the man selling felt so bad about it he came down considerably on his price. And you'd be surprised by the donations we've received this week. The story of our loss went all over the country and people are sending their support from as far away as California."

"And then there's probably insurance, too?"

"Maybe enough to buy us a new piano," he conceded. "Which reminds me. Our board's voted to send you a letter of thanks along with a letter to the Fire Department.

It means a lot to our congregation that you saved our pulpit Bible." He gave me a teasing smile. "And the fans, too, of course."

I grinned back. "My fifty-cent milk pitchers."

"Excuse me?"

So I gave him an abbreviated version of Daddy's tale of old Mrs. Crocker and how determined she'd been to save a worthless piece of china.

He nodded. "That'll happen."

As new arrivals bore down upon us, I said, "I hope your wife will be joining us later?"

"No, I'm afraid she doesn't feel well. She's subject to migraines and one caught up with her today."

He wasn't used to lying and I wondered what the real story was there. Unfortunately, I didn't have time to wonder long because I was immediately surrounded by friends and relatives and half the county's movers and shakers, each needing a hug or a handshake and some words of welcome or, since many of them had been at Mount Olive last Sunday, words of dismay about what had happened in Colleton County.

To my surprise, Wallace Adderly arrived with the Reverend Ligon.

"Hope you don't mind me crashing, Judge," he said with easy charm. "I hear your brothers are famous for their barbecue."

Early forties or not, Adderly had no gray strands in his close-cropped hair. I'd seen pictures of him back in his activist days when he wore his hair in an enormous Afro. Back then he'd been tall and whippet-thin with a feral

cast to his features. Now, he was broader of face and figure. Not fat, just matured to his fullest physical potential
through prosperity and regular meals.

"Delighted you could come," I assured him. "I'd have
sent you an invitation had I known you were going to
still be here."

"Oh yes," he said with pointed deliberation. "I'm
probably going to be here quite a while yet."

The pigs started coming off the grills at one o'clock and
Isabel and Aunt Sister got their hushpuppy assembly line
fired up. By one-thirty, Will and Robert had chopped
enough pork to get started.

We didn't have a podium per se, but my brothers and
sisters-in-law and I gathered together near the front tent
where Daddy was sitting with Luther and Louise Parker
and my cousin John Claude Lee, home from Turkey only
yesterday. When Daddy stood up and rang the hand bell,
everyone fell silent. Past eighty now, he was still straight
and tall and his soft white hair held the mark of the straw
Stetson he was holding in his strong hands.

"My family and I welcome you," he said. "It's always
a pleasure to us to have friends and neighbors join us like
this. I ain't much for making speeches—yeah, Rufus, I
hear you back there saying 'Good'—"

People laughed as Aunt Sister's husband held up his
wrist and tapped his watch.

"—and I ain't gonna let people who *are* good at making speeches talk till all the barbecue gets cold. But all
across this country, they's folks like you and me having

picnics and cookouts today and taking a minute to think about why we celebrate the Fourth of July. It's our birthday. The birthday of America. America don't always get it right and she's messed up pretty bad sometimes. But even messed up, she's still a lot better than anyplace else and we got to work to keep her that way. I ain't saying reelect my daughter and Luther Parker or reelect these county commissioners and Sheriff Bo Poole because America will fall apart if you don't, but it's people like them that does America's work and keeps her strong. Long as they're doing a good job in our little part of America, I say let's keep them!"

Loud applause, then Daddy called for everybody to stand and Annie Sue stepped forward to lead the singing of "The Star-Spangled Banner."

She and Louise Parker were probably the only ones who hit "And the rockets' red glare" dead on, but the rest of us made up in enthusiasm for what we lacked in ability.

More clapping.

"They's too many preachers here today for us to favor one over the other," Daddy said slyly, "so I'm gonna ask Judge Luther Parker to say grace."

Luther had evidently been primed, for he did ask God's help during these trying times and he did commend the soul of Arthur Hunt to God's mercy. Then he gave thanks for the day's fellowship and concluded by asking "that Thou bless this food to the nourishment of our bodies and our souls to Thy service. Amen."

Hearty amens echoed his and soon double lines were

passing down both sides of the serving tables where Minnie stood with a watchful eye, calling for fresh bowls of coleslaw or more hushpuppies as the baskets got low.

When I stopped to see if she needed any help, she had an infectious smile on her face. "Don't you just love watching people?"

"Who?"

"Second table on the left. Don't stare. Clifford Gevirtz and Alison Lazarus. He's wearing a yellow shirt, she's got on a blue dress. I said don't stare."

The woman looked vaguely familiar but I didn't recognize the man and certainly neither of them had Colleton County names.

"Who're Clifford Gevirtz and Alison Lazarus?"

"He's the new large-animal vet."

"The one that pulled Silver Dollar through colic this spring?"

Minnie nodded. "And she directs the literacy program here in the county. I introduced them last week and now here they are together. Don't they make a nice couple?"

"Matchmaking again, Minnie?"

"Well, why not? They're both from New York and they're both single and he's the best horse doctor we've had in a long time. *And* married men are more likely to stay put than bachelors. I do wish we could find somebody for Dwight Bryant."

Dwight was going through the line just then with a towheaded little boy in front of him.

"Hey, Cal," I called. "When'd you get down?"

"Hey, Miss Deborah!" A snaggle-toothed grin lit up his face. "My daddy came and got me last night."

Dwight's son and ex-wife lived in the western part of Virginia, a good five-hour drive away the way Dwight drives, but that doesn't stop him from making the trip whenever Jonna will let him have Cal for the weekend.

I broke line for a crisp hot hushpuppy and munched my way through hungry ranks to the table occupied by some of the courthouse crowd, including Cyl DeGraffenried, who didn't look overjoyed to be here. Clerk of Court Ellis Glover stood up with a half-eaten ear of corn in his hand and tried to give me his seat, but I motioned him back down and perched on the edge of my cousin Reid's chair as they hashed over the week's events yet again.

"—only thing saving us from the media sticking a microphone in our face every minute is no decent hotels out in the country," said Sheriff Bo Poole. "Keeps 'em in Raleigh." He sprinkled a few drops of Texas Pete hot sauce over his barbecue. "Keeps 'em there at night, anyhow."

"That and the quick arrest," said Magistrate Gwen Utley, blotting her lips with a paper napkin. "Knowing who did it takes the air out of their stories."

Reid was representing the Bagwell boy. He said nothing.

"You *are* going to plead your client guilty, aren't you?" asked Alex Currin, who, like me, is a district court judge and would therefore not be hearing the case.

"Hard to make a man plead guilty when he knows he didn't do it," said Reid.

"Yeah?" said Currin. "I heard they took a handwriting sample and Starling's printing matches what's on the church."

"Starling's not my client," Reid said.

"But your client says they were together that night," said Portland Brewer, and she reminded Reid of a story that had appeared in the paper only yesterday.

A reporter had gone back and researched the sale of Starling land some twenty-two years earlier, at least two years before Charles Starling was even born, to what became Balm of Gilead Church. He had spoken to contemporaries of Starling's grandfather, Leon, and he had pieced together a portrait of a hot-tempered alcoholic who used to run up huge tabs at various shot houses around the county. In less than fifteen years, the man literally drank up an inheritance of thirty-two acres and a crossroads country store back when you could still buy a farm for another four hundred dollars an acre.

Last to go was the land around the crossroads itself even though the store had been closed for several years. A devout black carpenter named Augustus Saunders had held the note on it for longer than any white bank would have, and when old Leon said he could have it for another five hundred dollars to finance what turned out to be his last alcoholic binge before his liver failed, Saunders took him up on it.

The store became a church and now the church was selling that parcel for almost a quarter-million. More than once in the past month, since word of the sale began leaking out, Charles Starling had been heard to curse Balm of Gilead and to swear that "a nigger stole my granddaddy's land for five gallons of white lightning" and "I'm owed, ain't I?" along with several other incendiary remarks.

Reid just shrugged. "I don't represent Charles Starling and my client had no grudge against any of those churches."

"Yes, but Bagwell—"

"Wait a minute—"

"*I* heard—"

As the others attacked, I stood up. "Anybody else want some fresh hushpuppies?"

Across the crowded tent, I saw Wallace Adderly making his way toward us.

Cyl DeGraffenried jumped to her feet. "I'll come with you," she said.

This was the first time she'd spoken to me directly since I found her crying in my office but I tried not to show my surprise. We picked up big cups of iced tea as we passed the drinks table and were halfway down the slope to where Isabel and Doris were frying up hushpuppies fast as they could when Wallace Adderly overtook us.

"Ms. DeGraffenried?"

I paused but Cyl kept walking.

"Ms. DeGraffenried!"

Without turning around, she said, "Yes?"

"Ms. DeGraffenried, have I done something to offend you?"

"Yes!" she snapped and continued walking.

I trailed along, just as puzzled as Adderly seemed to be, judging from the look on his face.

"When?" he asked. "What?"

Cyl stopped and turned and her eyes were as cold as the ice cubes in her tea. "You don't remember me, do you?"

"We know each other?"

"I know you, Snake Man." She fairly hissed the word.

Adderly did a double take, then shook his head. "I'll be damned! Little Silly. What's-his-name's baby sister."

"Niece," she snapped. "And his name is Isaac Mitchiner. My God! You took him into a snakepit and you don't even remember his name? He's dead, isn't he?"

❧ 16 ❧

CH CH
What's missing?
U R
  —*Plymouth Christian Church*

Wallace Adderly stared at Cyl as if she were a copperhead snake herself, coiled and ready to strike, and he unable to run. "I don't know what you're talking about."

"You know exactly what I'm talking about, Snake Man. Because of you, my uncle's gone. Because of you, my grandmother's grieved all these years. Because of you, she's never known what happened to him. But you know and you're going to tell her."

"What you talking, lady?" His usual cool had slipped away, revealing the wary, street-smart kid he'd once been.

"You think I was too little to understand and remember how you carried him off to Boston?" Cyl was almost rigid with anger.

"Boston?" Adderly asked blankly. Apprehension suddenly left his face and he nodded as if distantly recalling something almost beyond the reach of memory. "Boston. Yes."

People passing back and forth between the cookers and the tents gave the three of us curious glances but only Cyl's body language betrayed the intensity of the moment. She may have lost her temper, but she didn't lose control of her voice. Even enraged, her words were so low they could barely be heard above the clang of horseshoes against iron, the trash-talking kids at the volleyball net, and the lively buzz of a dozen or more conversations going on beneath the tents.

"Twenty-one years ago," she snarled. "You came through here. You with your big hair and your big head, spouting about injustice and oppression and how black power was going to change all that. All these years of seeing 'Black Advocate Wallace Adderly' in the news and I never realized you were Snake until last Thursday."

"I've never tried to hide my past," said Adderly, recovering his urbanity, slipping back into it like a fifteen-hundred-dollar suit. "I was here to mobilize this area. To register black voters. Isaac agreed with what I was trying to do and so did your grandmother."

"And look how you repaid her for taking you in, giving you a place to stay while you got Isaac stirred up. You helped him run off to Boston when he should have stayed here and straightened out his own life. If you'd left him alone, maybe he'd be here today. Maybe he'd be married now, with children of his own."

Her brown eyes glistened with unshed tears and I followed her glance to the laughing, dark-skinned little girl who went flying by like a swallowtail butterfly in an orange-and-yellow-striped bathing suit, yellow barrettes bouncing in the sunshine as she flitted away from Dwight's son Cal, who tried to tag her. It was Lashanda Freeman.

She glanced back over her shoulder to see how close he was, veered to elude him, and careened into Isabel, who was ladling hushpuppies from the deep-fat fryer.

Without thinking, Lashanda grabbed at the nearest object to keep from falling and her hand curled around the top of the cast-iron pot full of bubbling oil.

I watched in horror, expecting to see the whole pot come splashing over her, spilling hot grease that would fry that striped bathing suit right off her wiry little frame, but she was too small or it was too heavy. Even so, she howled in pain as her hand jerked away from the scorching iron.

Without thinking, I rushed over to her and thrust her small hand into my cup of iced tea. The only doctor out here was that veterinarian. Unless——? Atavistic memories clamored to be heard.

"Where's Aunt Sister?" I screamed at Isabel over Lashanda's screams. The girl's hand writhed against mine as I held it under the icy liquid.

Isabel pointed back up the slope toward the tents and I scooped the child up in my arms.

"Find her daddy," I told Cyl as I raced up the slope.

Lashanda was frantic in her pain, yet I couldn't run and keep her hand in ice at the same time and every second counted.

People hurried toward us, but I pushed through them. "Aunt Sister! Where's Aunt Sister?"

They pointed to the serving tent and there was my elderly aunt, Daddy's white-haired baby sister, fixing herself a plate of barbecue. She turned to see what all the commotion was about and as soon as I cried, "Burns. She burned her hand," Aunt Sister sat right down on the ground and held out her arms.

"It's okay, Lashanda," I crooned as I knelt to put her in Aunt Sister's lap. "She'll make the fire go away. It won't hurt much longer. Shh-shh, honey, it's all right."

Aunt Sister took the child's wounded hand between her own gnarled hands and bent her head over them till her lips almost touched her parted thumbs. Her eyes closed and I could see her wrinkled lips moving, but I quit trying years ago to hear what words she whispered into her hands when she cupped them around a burn.

"It's okay, honey," I said. "She'll take away all the fire."

Lashanda's terrified screams dropped to a whimper. Her brother came running and hovered protectively if helplessly while I continued to pat her thin bare shoulders and murmur encouragement.

"Feel the hot going out of your hand?"

She nodded, her fearful wide eyes intently focussed on Aunt Sister.

"Soon it'll be all gone. I promise you."

All around us, people watched with held breaths as Aunt Sister's lips kept moving.

Reverend Freeman burst through the ring, Cyl just behind him. "Baby—?"

He knelt beside us and put his arm around his daughter and she leaned against his chest with a little moan, but she didn't pull her injured hand away. "She's making it better, Daddy."

At last Aunt Sister raised her head and pushed back a strand of white hair that had escaped from her bun. Old and faded blue eyes looked deeply into young brown ones.

"All the fire is gone," she said. It wasn't a question.

Lashanda looked at her hand and flexed her small fingers. "Yes, ma'am."

Her palm and fingertips were smooth and unmarked. No blisters, only a faint redness.

A collective sigh erupted from the crowd and so many people started talking then that I was probably the only one who heard when Lashanda smiled up at her father and said, "Mommy's wrong, Daddy. These white people are nice."

I stood up, feeling suddenly drained and weary. A whole lifetime of knowing, yet I'm still surprised every time I get reminded that racism isn't a whites-only monopoly.

Someone handed me a welcome cup of iced lemonade. One of the newcomers, Alison Lazarus.

"Remarkable," said Dr. Gevirtz in a clipped New York accent. "I've heard of fire-talkers, but this is the first time I've ever seen it done."

"The colorful natives performing their ritual cere-monies?" I snapped. "Too bad you didn't have a camera."

"Was I sounding like a tourist?" he asked mildly. "Sorry."

Abashed, I apologized for my bad manners. "I'd be cu-rious and skeptical, too, if I hadn't seen Aunt Sister do it enough times."

"But surely it was putting her hand in cold liquid so quickly?" protested Ms. Lazarus.

"No, no," he said. "It's a true type of sympathetic heal-ing. The practitioner believes so strongly that those around her—especially the patient—also believe and that in turn causes—"

I excused myself and left them to it. I know all the in-tellectual arguments: the burn wasn't that bad, the prompt application of ice kept the tissue from blistering, the power of positive thinking, psychosomatic syndromes, et cetera, et cetera. As with old Mr. Randall, who dowsed my well, or Miss Kitty Perkins, who talked seven warts off my hands when I was fourteen, I no longer questioned how such things worked. It was enough to know that they did work, that there were people like Aunt Sister who had the gift and used it freely when called upon.

I was walking away from the tent when Ralph Freeman called to me, "Judge Knott? Deborah?"

"Yes?"

"I hope you didn't misunderstand back there."

"I don't think I did," I said evenly.

His eyes met mine and he nodded. "No, I reckon you didn't. I'm sorry."

"Don't apologize. We can't be responsible for everybody else's gut feelings. Your wife probably has better reasons than some of my relatives."

He gave a wry smile and we fell in step together.

"Must make it awkward for you," I probed.

"Not really." He walked along beside me with his hands clasped behind his back. "If you don't work outside the home, if you confine your social interactions to the African-American community, it's amazing how long you can go without having to speak to an ofay."

His voice parodied the offensive word and took the sting from it.

"School?" I asked. "PTA?"

The excitement over, the kids had resumed their volleyball game. We watched as Ralph's son took the setup and spiked the ball for another point.

"Sports?"

"Well, yes, there are those times," he conceded.

Despite a certain sadness in his voice, I sensed that he felt disloyal to say even this much about his wife and I quit pushing.

"Lashanda's okay?"

He seized gratefully on the change of subject. "Oh, yes. Ms. DeGraffenried—Cylvia? The prosecutor?—she took Lashanda up to your house to change out of her bathing suit and then there was some mention of a lemon meringue pie. I can't thank you enough for what you did."

"Not me. My aunt."

"She might have prayed the fire out, but you were the one got her to your aunt so quickly."

I shrugged.

Ralph Freeman stopped and smiled down at me, a smile as warm and uncomplicated as July sunshine. "You don't like to be thanked, do you?"

"Sure I do, but not when it's for something as elemental as helping a hurt child."

He brushed aside my demurral as if I hadn't spoken. "All you have to do is say 'you're welcome.' "

"Excuse me?"

"I say 'thank you,' you say 'you're welcome.' What's so hard about that?" There was such genuine goodness in his smile.

Goodness, and yet a touch of mischief, too, in the tilt of his head.

"Thank you for helping my baby girl," he said.

I smiled back at him.

"You're welcome," I said.

❧ 17 ❧

A trying time is no time to quit trying.
—*Jehovah Pentecostal*

Cyl soon returned with Lashanda, who had a flick of meringue on the tip of her little nose. For the child, getting changed had been a simple matter of sliding a pair of yellow shorts on over her bathing suit and stepping into a pair of yellow jelly sandals. She trailed an oversized yellow T-shirt across the grass and seemed too tired to walk.

Ralph Freeman swung her up on his broad shoulders so that a leg dangled down on each side of his chest and motioned to his son, who had just stripped off his rugby shirt and was ready to follow the other kids into the pond. The boy immediately put on a typical teenage face.

"Aw, Dad, do we hafta leave now? I didn't even get to swim yet."

I was amused to see that a preacher could be as torn as any father between the needs and desires of his children. Seven-year-old Lashanda was clearly exhausted and in bad need of a nap after such an emotional experience, while thirteen-year-old Stan was enjoying the swing of things.

"I don't mean to interfere," Cyl said hesitantly, "but if your son wants to stay a little longer, I could drop him off on my way home."

Stan's face lit up. "Can I, Dad? Please?"

"Are you sure it won't be too much trouble?" Ralph asked her.

"Positive. Just so Stan can tell me where you live. Cotton Grove, right?"

"Right," said Stan. "It's only two blocks off Main Street on this side of town."

"No problem then," Cyl said.

With a paternal injunction to behave himself and to come as soon as Ms. DeGraffenried called, Ralph thanked Cyl for her kindness and me for my family's hospitality. Then he headed out to the parking area with his daughter clinging drowsily to his head.

"Nice man," I said, watching them go.

"For a black man?" Cyl asked sweetly.

Stan had gone racing down the pier and we were alone for the moment beneath the hot July sun.

I felt as if I'd been spat on. "Excuse me?"

"Sorry," she said. "I spoke out of turn."

"But that's what you think?"

"I said I was sorry, Your Honor." She turned to walk away.

"Oh, no, no, no," I said hotly and grabbed her arm. "You're not getting out of it like that. Forget I'm a judge.

When did I ever give you a reason to lay something like that on me?"

"Woman to woman?" She looked me in the eye. "All right then. You show your prejudices almost every court session."

"Prejudices?" I was stung by the injustice of her accusation. "I bend over backwards to be fair."

An eyebrow lifted scornfully. "Right. You bend so far backwards when it's a black defendant that you go looking for mitigating circumstances even where there aren't any. You never hold black youths to the same high standard you hold whites. Oh, you're not as blatant about it as Harrison Hobart or Perry Byrd used to be, remember? Remember how they'd give suspended sentences if one black man killed another? Black-on-black crimes never got their attention. For them, it had to be black-on-white to put the law in play and then they came down like an avalanche."

"Now wait just a damn minute—"

She brushed past my protest. "I *said* you're not as bad as they were, but it's still condescending that you're always tougher on white boys than black ones. You're not doing them any favors when you don't hold them as accountable."

"How can you say that?" I argued. "I treat everybody the same."

"Ha! Maybe twice a month you'll hand out the sentences I recommend for a black offender," she said. "But if the person's white—"

"If anyone's condescending here, it's you," I said

hotly. "I don't follow your recommendations because they're consistently tougher than for whites. Go check your records. Look at the crime, not the color. See what you ask when it's a black kid as opposed to a white for the same offense. I'll bet you dinner at the Irregardless that I'm a hell of a lot more evenhanded than you are."

"You're on," she said with answering heat.

I was still annoyed enough to slip the needle in. "You ever consider that maybe it's your Uncle Isaac you're trying to punish for running out on you?"

She glared at me. "What do you know about Isaac?"

I shrugged. "Just what people have told me. That you loved him, that he got in trouble, and that you were devastated when he left and never kept in touch."

The belligerence suddenly went out of Cyl and she turned away. But not before I'd seen her eyes glaze with tears.

"I'm sorry," I said awkwardly. And I really was. But Dwight and my brothers are always accusing me of nosiness and I have to admit that it was curiosity that made me add, "Did Wallace Adderly tell you how to find him?"

"You may not have noticed," she said acidly, "but Wallace Adderly took advantage of Lashanda's accident to leave before I could pin him down."

I looked around blankly, but it was true. I couldn't see him anywhere in the crowd, although I did spot Reverend Ligon's tall figure standing in the shade of the tents with Louise Parker and Harvey Underwood, the president and major shareholder in Colleton County's largest independently owned bank. Harvey had already personally guaranteed a low-interest loan to help re-build the church. As Mount Olive's treasurer, Louise had set up a special account at the bank to handle the donations that were coming in from all over the country.

"Let me ask you something," Cyl said abruptly. "What was it like to grow up with all those brothers worshipping the ground you walked on?"

"Worshipping? *My* brothers?" I started to laugh and then I remembered the things Maidie had told me about Cyl's childhood. "They didn't worship, but I guess they did look out for me," I said as honestly as I could. "And I guess I always knew I could count on them."

"And what if you'd had only one brother and then he left and never came back?"

"Yeah," I said, seeing her point.

"Okay, then." She nodded and again started to walk away, but I followed.

"Look, Cyl, I don't know how we got off on the wrong foot, but I meant what I said the other day—if you ever need to talk, I'm here."

Again the skeptical eyebrow. "I could be your token black friend? As in Some Of My Best Friends Are Black?"

"If that's what you really want. And I can play Little White Missy From De Big House if it'll help with that chip on your shoulder."

"Oh, spare me your do-good liberal tolerance," she snapped. "I don't need it."

"Yes, you do!" I snapped back. "North Carolina may not be a black paradise but without a lot of do-good liberals trying to make things more equitable, you'd have had to take the freedom train north to get an education and you certainly wouldn't be prosecuting white offenders in a court of law here."

"And how long do we have to keep thanking you for letting us sit at the table?"

I'd thought—I'd hoped—things were getting better, yet here I was, looking at Cyl across a gulf that seemed to widen with every word.

"It's a no-win situation for me, isn't it? If I try to be friends, I'm either patronizing you or assuaging my own conscience; and if I don't, I'm a bigot. You get to have it both ways? What's so fair about that?"

"And you've been a judge how long?" she asked sardonically.

I laughed. It was the first crack in her armor.

"It started the summer I was four, when my cousins gave me the paper bag test and I flunked," Cyl said.

We had fixed ourselves plates of barbecue and were seated at one of the back tables. The first wave of guests had crested and Daddy and the rest of my family could handle host duties while I ate.

"What's the paper bag test?" I asked.

"Take an ordinary brown paper bag from any grocery store," she said, pulling apart a hushpuppy with her beautifully manicured fingernails. They were painted the same shade of coral as her soft, full-skirted cotton sundress. "Is your skin lighter or darker? You've seen my grandmother?"

I nodded, my mouth full of barbecue.

"And heard the rhymes? 'Light, bright—all right./ Honey brown—stick around./Jet black—get back.' "

"I've heard similar versions, yes."

"All of my mother's people were as light as Grandma. All except me. And her baby brother Isaac. He said we were the only true Africans in the family and we'd have to stick together."

She broke off. "This is crazy. Why am I telling you this?"

"My mother died when I was eighteen," I said.

"But your father didn't turn around the next month and marry a woman with three blond-headed Miss America daughters who sneered at your hair and put you down because your eyes are blue and not green."

I added a little coleslaw to the barbecue already on my fork. "I take it your stepsisters could pass the paper bag test?"

"They could almost do milk," Cyl said with a sour laugh. "I begged my dad to let me come live with Grandma, but he'd promised my mother—" She shrugged. "Just as well. While New Bern may not be the state's center of intellectual aspirations, at least my step-mother did believe in education. Grandma tried the best she could, but she was fighting against a culture here with lower expectations than New Bern, especially for its men. Even Snake Man couldn't get them stirred up and God knows he tried."

"Adderly?"

"That's what Isaac and I called him. He'd given himself a long African name that meant son of the snake god or something like that, but people kept remembering what it meant, not how to pronounce it, so by the time he got to us, it was just Snake. You should have seen him in those days. Bone skinny. Afro out to here—" Her graceful fingers sketched a balloon of hair around her own head. "—and army surplus fatigues. Don't forget, I was just a child back then, so all this time, I never connected the Wallace Adderly you see on television with the NOISE activist who zipped into my life and right back out again. Not until he popped up again on television after that first church burned."

"So *that's* why you were so upset in my office!"

She nodded and took a sip of iced tea. "Realizing who he was brought it all back again as if it'd just happened. Adderly was here only two or three weeks when he got a message that some of the brothers were going up to Boston. A federal court had ordered desegregation of the South Boston schools by forced busing and the Klan was supposed to be there, so NOISE planned a show of strength, too."

"And your uncle joined them?" I asked, slipping Ladybelle the second hushpuppy on my plate so I wouldn't be tempted. She gulped it down in one swallow and turned hopeful doggy eyes to Cyl, who heartlessly finished off the last of her hushpuppies without sharing.

"It was a rough time for Isaac," she said slowly, as she pushed her plate aside and laced her slender brown fingers around the red plastic drink cup on the table before her.

"I didn't understand all that was going on. Grandma had to tell me some of it later. Basically what it boils down to is that a lot of his pigeons came home to roost that summer. He'd gotten a deacon's daughter pregnant at the same time he was sneaking off to see a white girl with a mean brother."

"Anybody I know?"

"I forget her name. His was Buck. Buck Ferguson."

I vaguely remember a slatternly tenant family by that name that used to farm with Uncle Rufus before he got tired of bailing father and son out of jail. "Peggy Rose Ferguson?"

"I guess."

"Didn't her brother die in prison?"

"Wouldn't surprise me. Isaac said he saw him shoot a man in the arm over a spilled beer. You can imagine what he'd have done if he'd caught Isaac in the backseat of a car with that flower of Southern white womanhood he called his sister.

"Not that Isaac was any symbol of pure black manhood himself." Regret shadowed her voice. "He had a temper and he'd punched out a white boy, broke his nose. There's still a warrant for his arrest down at the court-house. He had so much rage in him. He wanted to marry the girl who was carrying his baby, but her parents sent her up North. They were going to make her give the baby up for adoption."

"Did she?"

"Who knows? She never came home again. I used to

fantasize that they found each other up there and ran away together."

"Maybe they did," I said.

Cyl shook her head. "He would never have stayed away all these years without calling or writing. No, he and Snake went to Boston and I figure he either got into another fight or was in the wrong place at the wrong time. I tried to trace him when I got out of law school, but after twenty years? And there was so much violence in Boston that summer. I used to think—"

"Hey now!" said Ellis Glover in his heartiest voice. "What's the two prettiest ladies at this barbecue doing sitting over here with such serious faces? I've been challenged to a game of horseshoes and I need a partner."

"Not me," Cyl said and quickly stood up. "Last time I tried, I broke three fingernails. Besides, I want to talk to Mr. Ligon before he leaves."

I could cheerfully have used Ellis's neck as a horseshoe stake at that moment for interrupting the first real conversation I'd ever had with Cyl. Would she retreat behind her armor again, embarrassed that she'd opened up to me? Pretend it never happened?

I didn't get a chance to find out that day. By the time Ellis and I beat two pairs of challengers and were then sat down by a third, Cyl had rounded Stan up and left.

And yeah, I broke a thumbnail.

❧ 18 ❧

Only God is in a position to look down on anyone.
—Westwood United Methodist

On Sunday, the *News and Observer* carried an in-depth report on the three burned churches: their histories, their significance in the black community, and how their congregations planned to cope with the loss.

Overall, the tone was upbeat. The Reverend Ralph Freeman explained that while the circumstances of Balm of Gilead's destruction were deplorable and much more precipitous than expected, the onetime service station was never slated to be saved once they vacated. "It has more than fulfilled its purpose and we assumed that Shop-Mark would simply bulldoze it when they began clearing the lot to build. In the meantime, we have an old-fashioned revival tent set up on our new site and we'd like to invite everyone reading this to put down their newspapers and come join us this morning to praise God for His goodness and everlasting mercy."

The *N&O* thoughtfully included directions to Balm of

Gilead's new location and a schedule of services. It also recapped how Leon Starling had once owned the old store and the land it sat on and how his grandson Charles was now charged with arson.

Like Balm of Gilead, Mount Olive was also finding mixed blessings in the fire. Previously, Reverend Anthony Ligon had been an enthusiastic, if diplomatic, advocate for expansion and he was almost ebullient when interviewed. He did his share of obligatory tongue-clicking, especially when it came to the tragic death of Arthur Hunt, whom they had buried Friday in a graveside ceremony, but his satisfaction came through more clearly than he perhaps intended.

"Our insurance policy covers replacement costs, not a set monetary value, so our fellowship hall with its Sunday School rooms will be re-sited. This gives us enough space to extend our sanctuary straight back and to double our seating capacity without damaging the basic integrity of the original sanctuary any more than the fire has already destroyed. From the outside it will look very much as it looked before the fire, except that the whole building will be somewhat longer."

The Historical Society had pledged to help find artisans to duplicate the dentil moldings and etched-glass windows. "We appreciate that this is a functioning church with modern concerns," said their spokeswoman, "but it is also such a historically important structure that we naturally want to do everything in our power to help preserve its architectural features. The slave gallery has been unsafe to use these last few years. We hope to raise funds to replace the old wooden supports with steel reinforcements."

Mr. Ligon confessed himself overwhelmed by the generosity of so many. "We've already been blessed with enough donations that we're hoping to begin clearing away the rubble this week. In the meantime, we're grateful to the County Commissioners and to the County Board of Education for giving us the use of West Colleton High's gymnasium on Sunday mornings. With God's help, we'll be back in our restored sanctuary before school starts again."

By contrast, the Reverend Byantha Williams sounded like the ill-tempered fairy godmother who crashed Sleeping Beauty's christening. While Burning Heart of God Holiness Tabernacle would be getting a pro rata share of any unrestricted donations designated to help "the three burned churches," it was not getting much sympathetic charity from the immediate neighborhood.

Sister Williams had neither the warm humanitarianism of a Ralph Freeman nor the political tact of an Anthony Ligon. Over the years, she had taken too much delight in pointing out the motes in the eyes of her fellow Christians—their sins of the flesh *and* their sins of the spirit. Their reluctance to come to her aid now only confirmed her sour view of them.

"You get back what you give," says Maidie.

There was no insurance on either the church or her small house trailer and the county had already warned her that she could not put another trailer back on the premises without a modern septic system. The old outhouse's proximity to the nearby branch was unacceptable, they said.

"God tempers the wind to His shorn sheep," she responded defiantly. "He will not lay on us burdens too heavy to bear. The sinner may not want to hear His message, but we will deliver it even louder. God has called me to call sinners to His holy cross and while there is breath in my body, I will not deny Him though the whole world denies me thrice before the cock crows three times."

The reporter seemed a little confused at this point, but put quotation marks around everything as if to deny his part in the confusion.

He reported that Burning Heart of God had been given the temporary use of an empty storefront in Cotton Grove (we later learned that Grace King Avery had persuaded a former student to make the offer) and that Sister Williams and her cats were living in the rooms behind it for the time being.

The article concluded by predicting that all three churches would rise, phoenix-like, from their ashes.

"Humph," said Maidie.

"Two out of three wouldn't be bad," said Daddy.

That evening, A.K. stopped by in his pickup on the way home after serving the second of his three weekends and asked if I wanted to go out for a pizza if I wasn't doing anything.

"Sure," I said, putting aside the case files that needed my attention and wondering what was up.

We drove out to a pizza place near the interchange.

"Everything's cool as far as jail's concerned, isn't it?" I asked as we pulled into the parking lot.

"Oh, yeah," he said. "No problem. It's not how I'd want to spend my life, but I can take one more weekend. What's going to happen with Charles and Raymond, though? They're in without bail. Will this count as their jail time?"

I assured him that if they were found guilty, they'd not be worrying about a few weekends in jail. "Assuming they don't get the death penalty, they'll be in a federal pen down in Atlanta and that's no stroll on the beach."

"Death penalty? You shitting me?"

I quickly briefed him on current laws and A.K. looked shaken as he held the door open for me.

The restaurant interior smelled of olive oil and hot yeasty dough. Even though he'd invited me, I had no illusions as to who'd be paying. We slid into a booth with padded red leather benches. He opted for the buffet; I ordered a salad (no dressing) and a slice with sausage and anchovies.

"The thing is," he said when he'd returned from the buffet stand loaded down with slices of pepperoni and green pepper pizza, "I don't think they did it."

"Charles Starling made threats," I reminded him, "and they don't have alibis."

"Aw, Charles." He gave a dismissive wave of his hand. "All front, no sides. He and Raymond can both be jerks—"

"So why do you hang with them?" I asked.

"Raymond helped us barn tobacco last summer. He's

okay. After Cathy and I broke up, he and Charles were tight and they weren't seeing anybody either."

"And Charles can pass for twenty-one at convenience stores?"

He gave a shamefaced nod. "Least he can at places where they don't look at your ID too close."

"Closely," I said automatically.

"Closely," he echoed, accustomed to his mother's corrections.

"Anyhow, the point is, Raymond didn't burn down any churches and neither did Charles. I got a chance to talk to Raymond today and he swore they didn't do it. They were at Charles's trailer when Mount Olive went up. From eight-thirty on."

"Unfortunately, no one saw them." I bit into my pizza slice. The crust was just as I liked it, and the anchovies went nicely with the mozzarella and tomato sauce.

"How can you eat them salty things?" A.K. grimaced at my enjoyment. "Anyhow somebody *did* see them. Somebody came over to borrow a backpack from Charles around nine o'clock."

"Why didn't this somebody come forward?"

" 'Cause he borrowed the backpack to go to some bass fishing tournament up in Massachusetts."

"Why didn't they speak up about it? Or tell Reid? He's Raymond's attorney."

"Thing is, Charles knows the guy's name is Jerry and his girlfriend's Bobbie Jean and he lives four trailers over, but he doesn't know either of their last names or where in Massachusetts they was going fishing." A.K.

twirled a string of melted mozzarella. "*Were* going fishing. And Charles didn't want to say anything till Jerry got back because Bobbie Jean was going with him."

"And?"

"And, well, it seems that Bobbie Jean's husband said he'd kill Jerry if he caught him messing around her again and Bobbie Jean sort of told her husband she was going to see her sister in Massachusetts and he doesn't know Jerry was going, too."

He popped the cheese in his mouth and looked around to see if the waiters had set out another pizza on the hot bar. This early in the evening, there weren't enough customers to merit a steady stream of fresh choices and he made do with two lukewarm slices of sausage and mushrooms.

"So, anyhow, Raymond's getting a little worried that what if Jerry comes back and Bobbie Jean's husband gets to him before he can come down to the police station and say they were there. So Raymond and me, we thought maybe you could tell Dwight and he could put out an APB or something and get to Jerry first."

I shook my head. "That's not going to happen, honey. In the first place, Dwight doesn't have jurisdiction here. It's a federal offense, not state. In the second place, it's Raymond's responsibility to tell Reid and then Reid will probably try to contact this Jerry, leave word at the trailer park for when he comes back."

"They didn't know whether the tournament was this weekend or next."

When I shook my head in amusement, A.K. said

huffily, "Well, jeez, Deb'rah. It's not like they knew they were going to need an alibi. Nobody thinks like that. Can you prove where *you* were between nine-thirty and ten o'clock last Sunday night?"

"As a matter of fact, I can," I said, remembering the long phone call Kidd and I had shared about then, he in New Bern, me lying across the bed with a report on DNA testing.

A.K. cut his eyes at me. "You gonna marry that game warden guy?"

I smiled. "I'll talk to Reid tomorrow, okay?"

"Yeah, but you still didn't answer my question."

"No comment," I said and signalled for our check.

❧ 19 ❧

One rowing the boat
Has no time to rock it
          —St. Catherine's R.C. Church

Monday morning's court was pretty heavy. Lots of misdemeanor possessions, assaults, a couple of B&E's, and a handful of check-bouncers. Cyl DeGraffenried prosecuted and she was as brisk and businesslike as ever as we moved through the calendar.

First up was a middle-aged black woman charged with writing two worthless checks to Denby's, a local department store. She waived counsel and pleaded guilty with explanation.

"See, what happened was I added up wrong and thought I had more than I did. And right after that, my sister's little boy had to have glasses and I loaned her the money I was going to use to pay the store back. She give me a check last Friday a week ago and I put it in the bank and wrote Denby's a new check, but my sister's check won't no good either. She was supposed to get me the cash money by first thing this morning, but her boyfriend's car broke down and he took her car to go to work, so she didn't have no way to come and—"

"Where does your sister live?" I asked.

"Near North Hills in Raleigh."

"And she has the full—" I checked the figures on the paper before me—"the full three hundred and five you owe Denby's?"

"Yes, ma'am."

"Plus eighty dollars court costs?"

"Yes, ma'am. I told her it was going to cost her four hundred for all my aggravation and she says she's got the money sitting there soon as she can get it to me."

"You have a car?"

She nodded.

"How long will it take you to drive to North Hills and back?"

"Two hours?" she hazarded.

"Let's make it three," I said. "I don't want you speeding. It's nine-fifteen now. If you're back here with the money by twelve-thirty, we can dispose of this today."

She hurried out, trailed by the accounts manager from Denby's.

Cyl DeGraffenried called her next case, Dwayne Mc-Daniels, 23, black. Dreadlocks and baggy pants. He pleaded guilty to driving while impaired and possession of a half-ounce of marijuana.

"What's the state asking, Ms. DeGraffenried?" I asked.

To my bemusement, she said, "Sixty days, suspended on condition he spend twenty-four hours in jail, pay a hundred-dollar fine and get the required alcohol and drug assessment."

"Let's give him the whole weekend to think it over," I said.

McDaniels was followed by Joseph Wayne Beasley, 18, also black, who pleaded guilty of driving while his license was revoked. Looking at his record, I would normally have given him a suspended sentence, maybe two weekends in jail and a five-hundred-dollar fine.

Cyl asked for the suspended sentence, one weekend in jail and a three-hundred-dollar fine and tried not to smirk when I held to my original assessment of appropriate retribution.

Robert Scott Grice, 24, white, pleaded guilty to assault on his girlfriend. To his attorney's visible dismay Cyl suggested he be sentenced to one hundred and fifty days in jail and not go near his girlfriend's house or place of work.

I gave him seventy-five with the same conditions.

It was like that all morning, Cyl asking lower penalties for black youths and higher for whites so that I had to toughen the one and reduce the other to reach a sense of fairness.

Just before noon, I motioned her up to the bench.

"Your Honor?" she said sweetly.

"Forget it, Ms. DA," I said just as sweetly. "Today does *not* count toward our bet."

She smiled. "So, when you want to do dinner?"

By noon, the ranks had thinned considerably and the courtroom held less than a third it had this morning.

The woman who bounced checks at Denby's had rushed through the doors a few minutes earlier, a thin glaze of perspiration on her dark face. She was now seated on the front bench right behind the bar. A crumpled white envelope was clutched in her hands and virtue shone in her eyes.

I motioned for her to come forward. "Your sister didn't let you down, did she?"

"No, ma'am, Your Honor. Here it is, every cent."

"I hope you didn't break the sound barrier, getting to North Hills and back," I said.

She chuckled and went over to my clerk to collect the necessary papers and then out to pay the cashier what she owed.

The Denby's manager looked pleased as he drew a line through her name on his notepad. There were still a bunch of names left though, more than would be appearing before me that day.

I recessed till one-thirty.

"All rise," said the bailiff.

The law firm of Lee and Stephenson, formerly known as Lee, Stephenson and Knott before I became a judge, is still located in a charming story-and-a-half white clapboard house half a block from the courthouse.

Robert Claudius Lee, John Claude's grandfather, was born there shortly after the Civil War, and so was Robert's brother, who grew up to be my mother's mother's father.

If you're Southern, you've already worked it out that

John Claude's my second cousin, once removed. If you're not Southern, you probably aren't interested in hearing that Reid is a cousin through my mother's paternal side, but no kin at all to John Claude.

Enough to know that John Claude's father and Reid's grandfather (my great-grandfather Stephenson) started the firm in this very house sometime in the twenties and that Lees and Stephensons have been partners there ever since.

Although both cousins have argued cases before me many times since I came to the bench, no one has yet accused me of favoring them. If anything, Reid's accused me of just the opposite. John Claude doesn't accuse. If he thinks one of his cases is going to be a hairsplitter, he manages to get it heard by somebody else, not me.

Although John Claude was arguing two cases in Makely that day, Reid was expecting me for lunch and I was expecting a quiet hour to catch my breath after such a busy morning with nothing much more weighty to discuss than Raymond Bagwell's alibi and whether we were actually going to get the thundershowers they were predicting on the breakfast news.

Instead, I came up onto the porch out of bright sunlight and when my eyes adjusted, I realized that Grace King Avery and Sister Byantha Williams were taking their leave of Reid.

Too late to run and nowhere to hide.

"Ah, Deborah!" exclaimed Mrs. Avery. "You know the Reverend Williams, don't you? Sister Williams, this is Judge Deborah Knott."

The elderly preacher was dressed in a pale green muumuu today. She was still a large woman, but her skin was no longer firmly rounded as in years past. It was as if her skin had stayed the same while the body beneath had shrunk two sizes. As we murmured acknowledgments, Mrs. Avery turned back to Reid.

"Is there any reason why Deborah couldn't give us an injunction right now? He needs to be stopped, Reid."

"Please, Mrs. Avery," he said rather desperately. "I promise you that I'll take whatever steps are necessary and feasible."

"Very well. If you're sure you understand the urgency of the matter?"

"I do, I really do," he assured her, and to me, "Come on in, Deb'rah."

It wasn't quite as blatant as yanking me inside with one hand and locking the door behind them with the other, but that's certainly what it felt like.

I hadn't stopped by in several months, so it wasn't surprising to see new carpets on the floor and new color on the walls. Julia Lee, John Claude's wife, is a frustrated designer and when she gets tired of redoing their personal house, she comes down and starts moving walls and ripping up carpets here.

My former office still sat empty. I haven't decided if that's because I'm irreplaceable or they figure I won't be reelected and will be coming back.

"Injunction?" I asked as I walked straight back to the rear of the house.

Several years ago, Julia had remodelled the old original kitchen. A tiny galley hidden by folding screens was at one end, the rest was a sunroom that could become a formal conference room or a comfortable place to spread out with morning coffee and newspapers.

Or lunch. The table was set for two and I knew that those waxed paper packets held creamy chicken salad sandwiches on homemade bread from Sue's Soup 'n' Sandwich Shop across from the courthouse.

Reid opened the refrigerator. "Tea? Or would you rather have Pepsi?"

"Pepsi, if it's diet. Who's got Mrs. Avery's feathers ruffled?"

"Guy named Graham Dunn, owns the Red and White Grocery and Hardware out from Cotton Grove." He put ice in two glasses and set them on the table beside the drink cans. "Seven years ago, Sister Williams signed a note with him for three thousand dollars."

"Using that raggedy old church as collateral?"

"That and the acre of land it used to stand on. The note came due last year, but he let it ride because it was clear she couldn't repay and he didn't want to look bad by closing on the church his parents used to attend."

Reid always jiggles the drink cans too much and some of the Pepsi foamed up when I pulled the tab. I mopped up the overflow with his paper napkin.

"But now that the church and trailer have burned?"

"Right." Reid unwrapped his sandwich, adjusted the lettuce and tomato and bit into it. His words were muffled as he talked around a chunk of chicken salad. "He's read the paper, seen that money is coming in from all over and figures this is his chance to clear her debt. Trouble is, when Mrs. Avery first called me yesterday, I called Louise Parker, who's overseeing the distribution of donations. She says they haven't yet received a single check made out to Burning Heart of God and what little undesignated money they have gotten will be prorated by membership."

I licked a fleck of chicken salad from my fingertip. "Burning Heart of God has what? Eight members? Ten?"

"Thirteen if you count one woman who hasn't left the nursing home in three years and a man who's serving a six-to-ten at State Prison."

"And did she borrow that three thousand as an individual or as an officer of the church?"

"As minister and chairman of the board of deacons, unfortunately."

"So he's looking to force a sale of the land and Mrs. Avery, full of noblesse oblige because of her grandfather King, wants you to stop it?"

"You got it."

"Can you?"

He shrugged. "I can try. I'll have to check the deed, see if it's in her name or the church's and then see if the church really is responsible for her debts."

He got up for more napkins. Sue's sandwiches are ambrosial, but messy to eat.

"You speak to Raymond Bagwell this weekend?" I asked.

"No." He handed me a wad of napkins and sat back

down across from me at the long conference table. "Is that what this lunch is about?"

I told him what A.K. had told me last night and watched the play of emotions across his face.

"Why the hell didn't my client tell me this?"

"Oh come on, Reid. As many times as you've taken married women to bed? I'd have thought you'd automatically understand the old male solidarity thing."

Not keeping his pants zipped outside of their bedroom is the main reason Dotty divorced him.

He gave a sheepish smile.

"Besides," I said. "Didn't you say Saturday that your client was innocent?"

"Yeah, but that's what I always—"

The penny finally finished dropping.

"If this alibi holds up—?"

"Yeah," I said. "It means the arsonist is still out there."

By the time I went back to court, he'd agreed that maybe A.K. wasn't wrong after all. Maybe Dwight *should* be told.

❧ 20 ❧

"Thou Shalt Not Steal"—Exodus 20:15
—Island Road Baptist

The storm that had been threatening all afternoon finally tore loose shortly before four-thirty as I was finishing up for the day. Lightning flashed, thunder crashed, a stiff wind tore leaves and twigs from the oaks that surrounded the courthouse and rain came down in such heavy sheets that when I looked out through the glass doors, visibility was less than a block.

Naturally I'd left my umbrella in the car.

"A real frog-strangler," commented Thad Hamilton as he came up and looked out over my shoulder.

Thad's one of the new breed. The first time he ran for county commissioner, he was a Democrat and finished far back in the pack. The second time around, he switched parties and became the first Republican elected to the county board in this century. He's about six-one, heavyset and, though only in his early forties, has a thick shock of prematurely white hair that makes his slightly florid face look even more youthful than it would have under ordinary salt-and-pepper.

"Sorry I couldn't make y'all's pig-picking, but I was at a fund-raiser for King Richard."

"We missed you," I said with sweet insincerity, "but I know Richard Petty's going to need all the money he can get if he actually wins the Secretary of State race—oh, but wait a minute! Didn't he say he was going to keep his STP endorsements, win or lose?"

"He won't lose," Thad said with the confidence of one who knows his man's ahead in the polls by double digits. "NASCAR champion versus that lady from Lillington?"

Never mind that Elaine Marshall was a sharp attorney and former state senator. As he travelled around the state, signing hats and T-shirts, Richard Petty couldn't seem to remember either her name or her title. It was always "that lady from Lillington." She talked of strategies to strengthen the office and better serve the state's business interests overseas; he didn't seem real clear on what the office entailed but was sure it was something that wouldn't take up more than three days a week.

Of all the Council of State candidates, she was the one I most wanted to win. Unfortunately, Thad was right. To most statewide voters, Elaine Marshall was a virtual unknown and King Richard knew how to win races.

"You've got an easy time of it this year," Thad said. "Running unopposed."

"Yeah, that sort of surprised me, too," I admitted. "I thought sure y'all'd put somebody up."

"We had bigger fish to fry this year," he said. "But don't worry. We'll get down to your level next time."

He unfurled a huge red-and-white-striped golf umbrella. "Walk you to your car, Judge?"

"Thanks," I said, "but I think I'll wait for it to let up a little."

Water was rushing across sidewalks and street too fast for the storm drains to handle it all and I knew that even if I shared Thad Hamilton's umbrella, my favorite pair of cork-heeled red sandals would be wrecked before I was halfway to the parking lot.

Fortunately, there was nowhere I needed to be until the Harvey Gantt rally out at the community college at six o'clock. Too, I hadn't really talked to Dwight on Saturday, so I took the back stairs down to the Sheriff's Department.

"Sorry, ma'am," said Deputy Jack Jamison. "Major Bryant and Sheriff Poole got called out to Mount Olive this afternoon and they're not back yet. I know he plans to swing by here before he goes home. Can I leave him a message?"

"If he gets back before five, tell him I'm in the Register of Deeds office," I said and went back upstairs to pester Callie Yelverton.

So far as we know, Miss Callie was the first Colleton County woman ever elected to a countywide office and she sort of got it by default since her daddy had held it from 1932 till his death in the seventies. (A county commissioner was the second and a school board member was third. I am the fourth.)

I had expected the records room to be empty, what with the rain and the late hour, but there were at least a dozen people busy with the big oversized books. I recognized a couple of attorneys' clerks, including Sherry Cobb, the office manager from Lee and Stephenson. Most of the others worked for the bigger developers. With the county's building boom, developers were knocking on kitchen doors all up and down every dirt lane, chirping, "Hi, there! Y'all interested in selling?"

I couldn't find anything in the index for Burning Heart of God, so I tried Byantha Williams. She was listed, but that particular deed book wasn't on the shelf, so I looked up Balm of Gilead instead.

Its origin was as the papers had reported: "Witnesseth, that said Leon Starling, in consideration of five hundred dollars and other valuables to him paid by Augustus Saunders, the receipt of which is hereby acknowledged, does convey to said Augustus Saunders and his heirs and assigns a certain tract or parcel of land in Cotton Grove Township, Colleton County, State of North Carolina, bounded as follows."

I wondered if the saintly Augustus Saunders had indeed thrown in the jug of moonshine that Charles Starling impugned him with.

A subsequent deed transferred that parcel to the board of trustees of Balm of Gilead Baptist Church.

Sherry spotted me and motioned me over. "Reid said you were there for lunch. Sorry I missed you." She was copying from the deed book that lay open on top of the waist-high bookcase in front of us.

"Is that the Burning Heart of God deed you're copying?" I asked.

"Uh-huh. Were you looking for it, too?"

She moved over a little so that I could read the simple deed in which Langston King did convey to Washington Renfrow "one acre upon which to build a Negro church. And should said church cease to exist or remove itself from that place, then the land shall revert to Langston King or, if he be dead, to his heirs and assigns."

Twenty-seven years ago, probably at the death of Washington Renfrow, another deed transferred title to Byantha Renfrow Williams, Chairman of the Board of Trustees for Burning Heart of God Holiness Tabernacle Church.

At this point, it could be argued that Sister Williams owned the church outright while an opposing attorney could no doubt argue that the church was a separate entity and owner of the land as implied in the original deed. Each would have a fair chance of winning the case depending on which way the wind was blowing or what day of the week Tuesday fell on.

"Technically, the church didn't remove itself," I mused aloud.

"But it's sure ceased to exist," said Sherry as she continued copying the deed's provisions in her rapid shorthand of hooks and curlicues.

"The building's ceased to exist," I agreed, "but the church itself is a body of worshippers, not walls and roof."

"You know, I never thought about it like that, but you're absolutely right. You see all you need to?"

I had.

As she slid the thick canvas-bound book back into its place on the lower shelf and went off to look up something else, I was left to think.

How about if Sister Williams declared Burning Heart of God legally defunct or else removed permanently to the storefront in Cotton Grove? She could let the land revert as specified in the deed and, since Mrs. Avery was the only surviving child of Langston King's only child, the land would then be safe from any immediate judgment. At that point, Sister Williams could declare bankruptcy and she'd have no assets a creditor could attach. If and when the church raised enough money to rebuild, Mrs. Avery could restore her grandfather's legacy.

"You're a judge now," the preacher inside my head reminded me. *"You're not supposed to give legal advice, remember? Besides, Reid's smart. He'll probably come up with the same idea."*

"And if he doesn't," said the pragmatist, *"you can always give him a little nudge tomorrow."*

"But what about the poor man who lent Sister Williams money? Declaring bankruptcy to avoid her debts is the same as stealing from him."

"His reward is in heaven," said the pragmatist.

Dwight was in his office and on the phone when I dropped by a second time. He motioned me in as he finished the call, hung up the receiver and leaned back wearily in his swivel chair. The chair was old and creaked as if it couldn't hold up under his six-three frame, but he didn't seem worried. He pulled the bottom desk drawer out with the tip of his boot and propped his size elevens on the ledge till he was nearly horizontal. His boots were caked with mud and so were the cuffs of his pants. His short-sleeved blue shirt was wet from the rain and there was a dark smudge on the shoulder.

I took the armchair across from him and saw the weariness on his face. He was supposed to have driven Cal back to Virginia yesterday and he'd probably gotten home late. "Rough day?"

"Yeah, you could say so. What's up?"

"Nothing much. Just wondered if you'd talked to Reid this afternoon?"

"Not yet." Dwight fanned some message slips with Reid's name on them. "You know what all these are about?"

"I probably ought to let him tell you."

"Probably. But all I'm getting is his answering machine, so why don't you go ahead and tell me yourself?"

Dwight listened in silence till I got to the part about Bobbie Jean Last-name-unknown being afraid of what her husband would do to Jerry Somebody if he found out they'd gone bass fishing together somewhere up in Massachusetts.

"Bobbie Jean Pritchett and Jerry Farmer."

"You know them?"

"Be nice if Bagwell had told us this before," he sighed.

"Before what?"

"Before Cecil Pritchett gave Farmer three broken ribs, a concussion, and a broken jaw."

"*What?*"

"Last night around nine. Pritchett made bail this morning. Farmer's over in Memorial Hospital. Bobbie Jean's hightailed it. Probably to her sister in Massachusetts for real this time."

"Can Farmer talk?"

"Could when he finally came to last night," said Dwight. "His jaw's wired shut right now, though."

"Can he communicate well enough to corroborate Bagwell's story?"

Dwight gave a palms-up gesture. "Who knows? I'll tell Ed Gardner, but I wouldn't count on him turning Bagwell and Starling loose anytime soon though. Starling might not've struck the match, but that's sure his printing on the walls."

"But if those boys didn't do it," I said, "you've got an arsonist running around loose."

"But if they did do it, we don't have to worry about any more fires right now. God knows we've got enough on our plate as it is."

"What?" I asked, realizing that he was more weary than a late drive home should have caused. "Something else has happened, hasn't it?"

He nodded. "Guess you might as well know. It'll probably be on the six o'clock news if it isn't already. They found another body out at Mount Olive."

❖ 21 ❖

LIVING WITHOUT GOD
IS LIKE DRIVING IN A FOG
—Nazarene Church

"Who is it?" I asked.

"We don't know yet," Dwight said. "At the moment, all we've got are charred bones."

That explained the dark smudges on his shirt.

As Dwight described it, work had begun today for Mount Olive's reconstruction. Two members of the church were bulldozer operators and a construction company had given them the use of some earthmoving equipment to clear the site. Others had volunteered to come help, too.

With that low pressure system moving in from the west, they were double-timing to get as much done as possible before the rains got here.

Starting at sunrise this morning, two big yellow bulldozers worked to push off the remains of the fellowship hall and send it to the landfill in heavy-duty dump trucks. By lunchtime, they were ready to start the more delicate operation of pulling off the burned parts of the main building, beginning with the old Sunday School classrooms and the choir stall where the sexton's body had been found. One forkload of burned choir benches and collapsed flooring went into the dump truck. When the second forkload swung up over the truck bed, a piece of debris fell from the air and landed a few feet from the man supervising the operation.

It was a leg bone.

The supervisor stopped the forklift in midair, took a look into the hole, and sent someone to call the Sheriff's Department.

"And we put a tarp over it, then called the Medical Examiner and the Feds," said Dwight. "Déjà vu all over again."

"You didn't recognize the body?"

"I wasn't exactly down there nose to nose."

"Male or female? Gunshot wounds or blunt trauma?"

"Give it a rest," he said with a big yawn. The chair creaked again as he sank deeper into it.

I thought of how hot it'd been all week and wrinkled my nose. "Must have been quite a stench."

He didn't bite.

Of course, he didn't just fall off the watermelon truck last week either. Before he and Jonna split, Dwight was with the D.C. police force and before that with Army Intelligence. I had the feeling he was holding something back, but he could keep his mouth shut when it suited him.

"The sexton was found in the choir loft, too," I mused.

"Wonder what they were both doing there? Hunt did die of smoke inhalation, didn't he?"

"So the ME says." Dwight yawned again.

"But he could have been hit over the head first."

"Not according to the ME. Alcohol level was point-nine-teen. Probably just passed out there," he said sleepily.

His own eyes were half-closed. Another minute and he'd be gone.

I was ready to go see if the rain had let up enough to get to my car when Cyl DeGraffenried suddenly appeared in the doorway. She wore a tailored rose-colored dress today with a string of white beads and low-heeled white pumps.

"I just got a call that a skeleton's been found at Mount Olive," she said. "Is that true?"

A skeleton?

I kicked the desk drawer shut and Dwight lurched forward so abruptly that the chair almost slid out from under him.

"You didn't say skeleton. You said body."

"A skeleton *is* a body," he protested, wide awake now.

Cyl had no patience for a battle of semantics. "How long?"

He didn't give her the runaround. But then she's an ADA, with more right to ask.

"At least three years. Probably a lot more. Near as we can tell, it was lying directly on the ground underneath the church. No burned material under it, but parts of both the original floor and the false floor had caved in on top of it. There was no flesh left. Not much clothing either, but that section was pretty badly burned. All we got were some half-charred shoes and part of a belt with a corroded steel buckle."

"In the shape of an M?" she asked harshly.

"M? We thought it was a W. You know who it is, ma'am?"

"Oh, Cyl," I whispered. "I'm so sorry."

She whirled around so fast that her string of beads swung out in an arc, then fell back into place with faint clicks as she half ran from the office.

I hurried down the hall after her.

"Hey wait!" Dwight called. "You know, too, Deb'rah? Who is it?"

His turn to wonder, I thought. Serves him right.

I caught up with Cyl at the elevator.

"You okay?" I asked, stepping into the car with her.

"No, but I will be soon as I talk to that lying s.o.b. Snake." She punched the button for the DA's office on the second floor. "I *knew* Isaac wouldn't go without saying good-bye. Wouldn't stay away without writing. He let me think Isaac went to Boston and all this time—"

Her voice wobbled and she shook her head, denying the tears that wanted to come.

On the second floor, I followed her down the deserted hallway to the equally deserted District Attorney's quarters. She hauled out a phone book, turned to the motel listing and dialed the number for the Holiday Inn out at the bypass where she asked to be connected with Wallace Adderly's room.

I couldn't hear the other side of the conversation, of course, but it was easy enough to follow.

"Well, do you know when he'll be back? . . . Is he registered for tonight? . . . Thank you very much. . . . No, no message."

She hung up with a muttered, "Damn!" and then tried the Reverend Ligon's number.

Answering machine.

Another frustrated hangup.

Hesitant to play devil's advocate, I said, "When you talked with Adderly Saturday, he didn't actually say Isaac went to Boston with him, you know. You're the one mentioned Boston."

"You didn't hear him deny it, did you?"

"Well, no, but coming out of the blue like that? He's a political animal. He wouldn't speak without weighing all the ramifications."

She continued to riffle through the phone book, then slammed it down on her desk. "I can't think where he'd be in this one-horse town. Maybe Raleigh?"

Angrily, she reached for the book again.

I glanced at my watch. 5:45.

"You up for more barbecue?" (In the North, it's the chicken and hot dog circuit; in the South, it's barbecue—endless plates of hushpuppies, coleslaw and vinegar-laced barbecue.)

My question caught Cyl off balance. "Barbecue?"

"The Harvey Gantt rally," I reminded her. "Out at the community college."

"Adderly's supposed to be there?"

"So far as I know, that's the only thing happening tonight that would bring him out."

Cyl nodded, then looked at me helplessly as the grief that had been building suddenly crumpled her lovely face. Her dark eyes pooled with tears that spilled onto her rose-colored dress, making little dark wet spots.

"All this time he was right here," she said brokenly, reaching for the box of tissues behind her. "Never got out of Colleton County. Never had a life."

Sometimes, the only thing you can do is just put your arms around a person and hold on tight.

"Are you sure you wouldn't rather try to catch him after the rally, back at his motel?" I asked Cyl as we drove through town.

I had convinced her that she shouldn't be driving alone in the rain in her emotional state, but I couldn't convince her to go back downstairs and tell Dwight everything she knew or suspected.

"I've waited twenty-one years to know what happened to Isaac," she said fiercely. "I'm not waiting any longer."

Colleton County Community College had begun life back in the mid-fifties under Governor Luther Hodges as part of the state's string of technical and vocational schools designed to give rural kids a chance to learn a trade or pick up two years of college credits on the cheap while living at home.

It was still raining on Harvey Gantt's parade when we

got there, but the organizers had rallied their forces and regrouped.

Instead of a pleasant picnic supper in the oak grove next to the administration building as the sun went down, the pig cookers had been moved out of the rain to the other side of the building where a wide covered walkway connected to the auditorium. There, a spacious lobby accommodated buffet tables, and a podium backed with red, white and blue bunting stood waiting at the far end. Also waiting were a couple of television cameras. This was Harvey Gantt's first visit to Colleton County since the burnings and reporters would be wanting his reaction to events, no matter how predictable that reaction would be.

Gantt was a man of solid Democratic values and he probably would make a pretty decent senator given the opportunity, but he lacked that fire in the belly that would let him get down in the mud and wrestle with Jesse Helms on Jesse's level, so I didn't have good vibes about his chances this time around either.

But optimism springs eternal in a yellow dog's heart and I hoped the thin crowd was more reflective of the rain than of Gantt's following. Although soggy gray skies could be seen through the clear skylights overhead, someone had turned on all the lights to brighten things up.

Minnie and Seth waved to me from across the lobby. I shook the worst of the rain from my bright yellow umbrella, raised it to furl it closed and wound up fencing with someone doing the same thing.

"En garde!" I said and Ralph Freeman laughed as he snapped the tab on his and stood it in the corner where other umbrellas were dripping.

"Lashanda and Stan weren't up to more barbecue?" I asked, adding mine to the lineup.

"They'd eat it every day," he said, "but my wife's taken them to visit her parents back in Warrenton for a couple of weeks and I'm not all that crazy about my own cooking."

His smile broadened to include Cyl. "Ms. DeGraffenried. I hope Stan told you how much he appreciated you driving him home Saturday?"

"Your son has impeccable manners," she said. She stood on tiptoe and scanned the crowd, which seemed to be growing as classes broke and the smell of roast pig floated across the campus.

"I don't see him."

"See who?" asked Ralph.

"Wallace Adderly."

"Just look for the flash of cameras," I said and pointed toward the front.

Sure enough, Harvey Gantt and Wallace Adderly were sharing media attention up at the podium. Print and television were both there and I recognized the kid who worked out at the AM station on the edge of town. He had a microphone stuck in Adderly's face and even from here, body language told me that the attorney was answering earnestly and graciously.

I followed Cyl across the width of the lobby, though I

was slowed by more people putting out their hand to me for a word of greeting.

As we came up, a pretty young reporter from WRAL must have just asked Adderly a question about quotas because I heard him say, "—new right-wing buzzword. I believe in merit and a fair chance for everyone and in a perfect society there would never have been a need for quotas. You're too young to remember when the quota for African-Americans was zero. And for women who wanted to report on-camera," he added, flashing her his famous charming smile, "it was less than zero."

As he turned toward the next questioner, Cyl stepped between them and spoke into his ear. I don't know what she said to him—"My Uncle Isaac's bones have been found"?—but whatever it was, he excused himself with another smile, quickly took her by the elbow and led her through a nearby door to a covered areaway outside.

I was right behind.

Adderly gave me an annoyed glance. "Could you excuse us, Judge? This is a private matter."

"I'm her friend," I said above the dripping of the rain.

For some reason Cyl seemed even more surprised by that than Adderly.

"Besides," I added, "if you had anything to do with Isaac Mitchiner winding up under the floorboards of Mount Olive, it's not going to stay private very long."

For just an instant, Wallace Adderly looked as if he'd been sucker-punched. He recovered instantly though and said, "Look, is there somewhere we can go talk?"

"Need time to get your new story straight?" Cyl asked.

Nevertheless, she looked around vaguely as if expecting to see a place open up.

"This way," I said.

While still in private practice with Reid and John Claude, I had come out here to speak to various paralegal classes—this is where Sherry Cobb got her training—so I knew a bit of the layout.

A quick splash down a bricked walkway took us to an unlocked door and the stairwell of a classroom building. At the top of the first flight was a small study lounge that was usually empty. We went inside, I flipped on the light and closed the door behind us. Inside were a black leather couch, three leather armchairs and a badly scuffed coffee table in between, handy for books, coffee cups or feet. A single window overlooked the front of the auditorium, where people were lining up with their plates for servings of the chopped pork.

Adderly took one of the armchairs, Cyl another. I opted to perch on the window ledge. To Adderly's annoyance. For some reason, he seemed to think I was the one he had to worry about.

He didn't realize that Cyl was no longer the trusting little Silly he remembered and her question came like a whiplash across his face. "Why did you kill him?"

"Hey, now, wait a minute here," he protested. "A judge and a DA? Maybe I ought to have an attorney present."

"You tell her what she needs to know," I said, "or I guarantee you'll be hearing the same questions from those reporters down there before you can get out of the parking lot. And 'No Comment' always sounds so much like 'nolo contendere,' don't you think?"

He took a long moment to consider. "What I say stays here?"

I looked at Cyl but I couldn't read her eyes.

"You're an officer of the court," the preacher reminded me.

Alarm bells were going off for the pragmatist, too.

"You're stepping in quicksand here," he warned.

I took a deep breath. Trust had to start somewhere. "It's her call," I said.

"Weird," Adderly said at last. "I spend twenty years staying out of Colleton County and the first time I come back?" He shifted in the chair and crossed his legs.

"What you have to understand is that things weren't bad enough here. I never understood why the leadership sent me here in the first place. Yeah, this was Klan country—used to be big signs on both sides of Dobbs bragging about it, but not like other parts of the South or even parts of the North where we'd been ground down so far there was nowhere to go but up, nothing more to lose if we stood up for our rights. Desegregation had gone smoothly enough here. You had the usual prejudice and casual bigotry that's still around today, but it wasn't organized and systematic and black people here *did* have something to lose. They didn't appreciate outsiders like me coming in to rock the boat, either.

"In two weeks, I maybe persuaded ten people to register to vote. 'Course, it might've been me, too. I was getting frustrated with NOISE. Seemed like all the effective action was happening somewhere else.

"All the same, when word came down to get my butt up to Boston 'cause they were expecting violence with the new busing regulations, I just couldn't get revved up for it. Isaac though, he would've caught the next Greyhound out of here if he'd had the money and a place to go. He wanted to leave in the worst way. You knew that?"

Silent tears ran down Cyl's smooth brown cheeks as she nodded.

"I'm sorry," Adderly said, "but I didn't create the situation. There was a girl he loved, daughter of a preacher or an elder or somebody else whose shit didn't stink, if you'll forgive my crudeness. Her parents were dead-set against him so he got her pregnant, figuring they were so respectable they'd have to allow a wedding so that the baby wouldn't be a bastard. Instead, her mother sent her somewhere up North to have an abortion."

"Abortion?" Cyl looked shocked. "My grandmother said the baby was supposed to be given up for adoption."

"That was what he let your grandmother think. Truth is, the girl's mother told Isaac that he was about ten shades too dark. No daughter of hers was going to marry back into Africa or have his pickaninny baby either. Those where her exact words.

"Isaac was hurting so bad, he took up with some white girl just to prove he could. 'Too black for a black girl, just right for a white.' That's what he told me. He knew she came from a rough family, but he didn't care.

"Her cousin threatened to tell her brother and Isaac broke his nose with a two-by-four."

Adderly stood up and walked over to the window where I was and stared down at the crowd that was laughing and talking and digging into the barbecue. He stood there for a long minute, then walked away. There was barely room to pass between the coffee table and the couch and the room wasn't really long enough for pacing, but somehow he managed.

"It was all coming down on him and he begged to come to Boston with me."

"Why didn't you let him?" Cyl asked harshly.

"Girl, you forgetting the times? The circumstances? You think I had what I have now? That Isaac had two quarters to rub together?" He made another restless circuit of the room. "All he had was your grandmother's generosity and some odd jobs he picked up in the neighborhood before barning season started. All the same, I did tell him that if he could get together the money for a bus ticket by the time I was ready to leave, I'd take him with me. There was no sexton at Mount Olive back then and they'd hired Isaac to do the yard work once a week. I walked over to help him that afternoon because I'd decided to leave for Boston the next day and I hoped that if he couldn't come with me, maybe he could keep up the work, try to get out the vote that fall."

His constricted pacing put my nerves on edge but Cyl sat motionless.

"He was cutting the grass when I got there, so I went back to what used to be the storage room, picked up the pruning shears and starting trimming that row of shrubs around back. I didn't even realize anybody'd come up till I heard the lawnmower shut off and car doors slam, then loud male voices. I walked down to the corner and peeped through the bushes. There were five white men. Two had grabbed Isaac and a big guy was hitting him and yelling about his sister. Then he punched Isaac in the chest—right on the heart, I'd guess—and Isaac just sort of folded over like a rag doll.

"The two guys holding him let go and he fell on the ground and one of them said, 'Jesus, Buck! You've killed him!' And Buck said he was faking, but the other guys were running back to their cars so Buck ran, too."

He paused, as if expecting Cyl to speak.

She didn't say a word. Just looked at him so steadily that he had to turn away.

"Okay, yeah, but that was twenty-one years ago. Easy enough now to say I should have gone running to the white sheriff and told him about five white guys I'd never seen before killing a black kid. I was a NOISE activist, for God's sake! You think they'd take my word against theirs? And if I just walked away and headed for Boston, it would have been real easy for the white authorities around here to find a dozen reasons to come after me for Isaac's death. I wouldn't even have known who Buck Ferguson was if he hadn't kept yelling about niggers fucking his sister.

"All I could think of was getting the hell away without getting involved. I carried him into the storage room, then I got the mower and clippers and stuck them there, too.

The room was just sheets of plywood nailed to two-by-four studs. I took a hammer and pulled one of them off and got Isaac into the crawl space under the church. I pushed him as far in as I could, back to a part that didn't have any electric wires that people might have to get to. There wasn't much room to dig, but I managed to scoop out a little hollow and cover him over and that's where I left him. Your grandmother didn't say much when he did-n't come home that night. It wasn't the first time."

Even with air-conditioning, the little lounge was be-ginning to feel hot and humid. Beads of perspiration stood out on Adderly's face and he took a handkerchief and wiped them away.

"Next morning, I don't know if you remember, but you and your grandmother and your cousins went off to pick dewberries for a truck farmer down the road?"

Cyl shook her head.

"Well, you did. Which was a good thing, because lying in bed that night, I realized I hadn't thought of something. Then I remembered seeing a dead hound out by the side of the road—a big stray that got hit by a car. After y'all left that morning, I found a burlap sack in your grand-mother's garage and I waited till the road was clear and stuck the dog in the bag and carried it through the woods to Mount Olive.

"There were sacks of quicklime in the storage room—that stuff they used to sprinkle down the hole to keep out-houses smelling sweet? I layered a whole sack of it over Isaac's grave, then I made a little hole in that lattice skirt-ing at the back of the church behind the shrubs and

pushed the dog through it. I figured if the quicklime did-
n't do the whole job, they'd find the dog first and think it
crawled up under there to die and they wouldn't look any
farther.

"Afterwards, I went back to the house, packed up my
clothes and a few things of Isaac's so y'all would think
he'd gone with me, then I hitchhiked into Raleigh, cashed
in my bus ticket to Boston and bought another one home
to Wilmington."

"Where you quit NOISE, studied for the bar and
started preaching about people needing to take responsibility for their actions," Cyl said.

"Makes me sound like a hypocrite, I know," said
Adderly. "But if I preach, it's from experience. Not a day
goes by that I don't think about Isaac and feel ashamed
because *I* didn't take responsibility for bringing his killer
to justice. Maybe after all these years, we can find the
men who held him down. Maybe they're ready to accept
their part in it and testify against Buck Ferguson."

"Very noble," I said. "And I suppose you're willing to
tell the Sheriff your part in all this and testify, too?"

"If that's what it takes," Adderly said.

"Even though Buck Ferguson died in prison at least
eight years ago?"

"What?"

Most good lawyers are actors and Adderly's certainly a
good lawyer. Even so, his surprise looked genuine to me.

So did the expression of relief that immediately followed.

╪ 22 ╪

Praying hands
Aren't preying hands
—Sandy Hill United Christian

"So what are you going to do, Ms. DeGraffenried?" Adderly asked. "March out there and throw me to those reporters?"

"No," Cyl said slowly. "Destroying you doesn't bring Isaac back."

"You're going to keep quiet about this?" I asked indignantly.

"You said it would be my call."

"But you're letting him get away with—"

"—with what exactly?" Cyl interrupted sharply. "He didn't kill Isaac."

"So he says now."

"He had no reason to kill. And as for hiding his body and running away, there's probably a statute to cover it, but I don't know what it is off the top of my head. Do you?"

"No," I admitted, although preacher and pragmatist

were both frantically flipping through all the cases filed at the back of my skull.

She gave an impatient twitch of her shoulders. "If anything, it's probably just a misdemeanor that the statute of limitations ran out on years ago."

I shook my head. "Hiding a body and covering up a violent death? That's more than a misdemeanor, Cyl. We're talking felony here and there's no statute of limitations on felonies in this state."

When I'd said it would be her call, it was because I'd been so sure she'd go by the book. I had no grudge against Adderly, but neither was I ready to sacrifice my career for him and no way did I like where this situation was headed. Cover-ups are stupid and they never work if more than one living person knows what's being hidden.

Somewhere a little bell went off, but Cyl made it hard for me to hear.

"Prosecute him for that? What's the point? Isaac's still dead, the man that killed him is dead, his accomplices scattered and even if we could round them up, the worst we could charge them with is involuntary manslaughter."

Smart enough to know that any comment by him might tip the balance scales of justice either way, Wallace Adderly watched us silently, motionless except when his dark eyes shifted from Cyl's face to mine and then back again as we argued it out between us.

"You're willing to risk censure if this comes out?" I asked her. "And what about your grandmother? Is she this forgiving?"

"My grandmother admires the man he's become," Cyl

said stiffly. "She doesn't know that he's the same person who stayed in her house twenty years ago."

"And if she did know?" I persisted.

Her voice hardened with scorn. "You whites can pull a leader off his pedestal every time you notice a clay foot because you've got a whole row of men waiting to take his place. We don't have that luxury. Our leaders have been bombed and shot and lynched and I'm sorry, but I'm not ready to help this culture destroy another one just because he panicked and did something stupid before he was fully mature. Something he could have denied till the day he died, if he'd wanted to, because who could prove anything? You? Sheriff Poole? Doug Woodall? *I* certainly couldn't and I was there."

The little bell was ringing like a fire alarm as the pragmatist tried to get my attention. Something about Wilmington stirred in my memory. Adderly was from Wilmington. Was that it? . . . No, not Wilmington exactly . . . but something that happened in the Fifth Judicial District? Pender County? No. It was something I'd heard about when I was *in* Pender County. *Yes!* A Wake County ruling? Something about a fire and someone confessed to setting it, but his conviction was vacated because—

"Well, I'll be damned!" I said as I finally remembered.

They both stared at me.

"You're right, Cyl. It's a naked confession and an uncorroborated, extrajudicial confession cannot sustain a conviction. I forget the case but we can look it up. No witnesses, nothing to show how your uncle died, no evidence of manslaughter, no way to prove or disprove any felonious acts, including how he got under the church. *Nada*."

I gave Adderly a congratulatory tip of my imaginary hat. "Lucky you. Nothing worse than a small PR problem if rumors should start."

Cyl shook her head. "It's not a complete pass. I guess I do have to tell my boss even if there's nothing official he can do. And you," she said to Adderly, "have to tell my grandmother."

"Yes," he agreed. "I owe her that."

"How quiet it stays is up to them. And to Judge Knott, too, of course." She gave me an inquiring look.

"Your call," I said again, feeling better about it this time, now that some solid legal ground had appeared beneath that ethical quicksand.

Cyl stood then and smoothed the wrinkles from her linen dress. "I'll be in touch."

He nodded and the last of my indignation dissipated.

I'd been flippant about the damage to his reputation, but Cyl was right. It would be a real waste if the act of a scared young man twenty years ago did indeed damage the reputation of the leader he'd become.

Isaac Mitchiner wasn't the only victim here.

Rain was still falling when we left the building and scurried over to the covered portico in front of the auditorium.

Ralph Freeman was just coming out with his umbrella in hand and he shook his head as we drew nearer.

"I can understand why you might skip the political speeches, but don't tell me you aren't eating either?"

"Hungry?" I asked Cyl. "Or do you want to leave?"

She shook her head. "Don't take this wrong, Deborah, because I do appreciate what you did, the things you said, but—" She turned to Ralph. "If you're ready to go, Reverend, would you mind giving me a lift back to the courthouse?"

"I'd be glad to." He opened his umbrella and held it over her.

I watched them go and yes, damn it, I *was* taking it wrong . . . if feeling as if I'd been slapped was taking something wrong.

"She didn't mean it personally," said Adderly, who had come up behind us and witnessed the whole scene. "Sometimes being with whites is just too stressful."

"Now you're going to argue for reverse segregation?" I asked.

"No, but I wouldn't mind if white folks could appreciate that it isn't a one-way street, that integration brings losses for us, too. I'm never going to quit working for a North Carolina where all blacks can feel comfortable everywhere, no matter who's sitting at the table with us—a North Carolina where we can quit having to be a credit to our race every minute of every day because there's always some honky ready to say 'Ain't that just like a nigger?' if we aren't. But until that happens, there have to be times and places where we can sink down and lay our burdens aside and know for sure that nobody's sitting in judgment but God."

"Black churches," I said.

He nodded. "And black friends."

I could see his point, but bedamned if I had to like it.

Disconsolately, I stepped inside the lobby to retrieve my umbrella just as Reid was coming in. He grabbed my arm with a big smile.

"Hey, Deb'rah! Sherry said you saw Langston King's will, too. Guess what?"

"Sister Williams is going to let the land revert?"

His face fell. "How'd you guess?"

"Just a wild stab."

"I drove over to Cotton Grove—the rain was coming down in buckets, too—and explained it to Mrs. Williams and then she and I went to see Mrs. Avery. She didn't know about the reversion clause and she wasn't real sure it was the right thing to do, Mrs. Avery, I mean. We really had to sell the idea to her and then she and Mrs. Williams had to pray on it awhile before she finally agreed. We're going to start the paperwork first thing tomorrow morning."

"That's nice."

"Hey, you okay?"

"I'm fine."

"You look a little down."

"It's the weather. And it's been a long day."

"I don't suppose you got a chance to talk to Dwight?"

"Actually, I did," I said. "Unfortunately, half your client's alibi is over in Dobbs Memorial with his jaw wired shut and the other half's on her way back to Massachusetts."

"You're kidding."

"Trust me. I'm not," I said and related what Dwight had told me earlier that afternoon.

He listened intently, shaking his head in dismay. "I'll see if we can get a court reporter there tomorrow to take his deposition."

"It's none of my business," I said, "but if it were me, I wouldn't be in too big a hurry about this."

"How come?"

"Dwight may want to believe that Starling and Bagwell set those fires, but he won't disregard a solid alibi and last night's beating ties in with the story A.K. told me at least three hours before the beating occurred. Give him a chance to convince himself and Dwight'll turn around and convince ATF. Bet you a nickel he'll have talked with Jerry Farmer and Bobbie Jean Pritchett, too, by tomorrow night."

"Bet," said Reid. "And I hope I lose."

❧ 23 ❧

Real angels never look for the angles.
—Booker Grove Methodist Church

If I'd found him, I probably could've collected my
nickel from Reid when I broke for the afternoon recess
the next day.

As I crossed the atrium that connects the new part of
the courthouse with the old 1920s part, I almost banged
into a hefty young white man who began with an apology
and ended with a pleased smile on his face. "Judge Knott!
Glad to see your hair's none the worse for all those
sparks."

It was the volunteer fireman who'd hauled out the pulpit on one shoulder the night Balm of Gilead burned.

I fumbled for his name. "You're Donny, right? Donny
Turner?"

"Yes, ma'am," he beamed, "and I owe you an apology.
I didn't know I was ordering around a judge that night."

"No problem," I said. "How's it going?"

"Just fine. Hey, maybe you can help me?"

"Sure. What do you need?"

He took a crumpled slip of paper from his jeans pocket. "I got a call to come see Special Agent Ed Gardner? In Major Dwight Bryant's office? You happen to know where that would be?"

"Well, you could have gone in directly from the street behind, but there's a staircase. Let me show you."

I led him through double glass doors, along a wide hall, down the stairs and through another set of glass doors. As we walked, Donny Turner kept up a running chatter on why he was there. He didn't seem to be completely sure.

"I reckon they want to get an in-depth report of what it was like when them churches was actually burning? From one of the troops? Somebody as was right there, don't you reckon?"

"You were at all three?"

"Well, not that little one with the trailer. Burning Heart of God? Boy, that was a real appropriate name, won't it? Naw, none of us got to that one. We was all at Mount Olive, working on that fire, when the little 'un went."

Donny Turner's Colleton County accent was as thick as Daddy's—wasn't is always *won't*, fire is *far*—and he was bad for making every other sentence sound like a question, but I grew up on those sounds and I've never needed a translator.

"Did you know Charles Starling or Raymond Bagwell?" I asked.

"Oh, sure. Charles, anyhow. He was a year behind me but we rode the same school bus and we carpooled after I got my license. Till he quit school? Man, you could have knocked me over with a feather when I heared he was the one done it."

"Really?" I halted on the stairs and stared at him.

Surprised, Donny stopped, too. His eyes met mine briefly, then darted away. "Well, no, I guess not really. He was sorta wild in school, always breaking the rules? He was the one spray-painted our bus when we was in middle school? And you know his momma kicked him out of the house 'cause he kept burning holes in everything with his cigarettes and I heared he was real mad with Balm of Gilead 'cause they stole his granddaddy's land?"

"Yeah, that's what I heard, too," I said.

"Maybe that's how come they want to talk to me? 'Cause I know Charles could've done it?"

Again his eyes shifted away. Nervousness?

"Ed's and Dwight's problem, not yours," said the preacher.

"But you can call Dwight this evening," said the pragmatist. *"See if he wants to watch a movie."*

We entered the Sheriff's Department through the glass doors. "Right around that corner," I told Donny Turner. "Major Bryant's office is the second door on the left."

At that moment, a familiar person rounded the corner.

"Hey, Chief!" said Donny. "They got you down here, too?"

"Uh, yeah, well, you know how it is."

Was it my imagination or was the chief of West Colleton's volunteer fire department having trouble looking Donny Turner straight in the face?

"I'd better not hold y'all up," he said, giving me a nod as he passed. "I believe they're waiting on you, Donny."

"Yeah, okay. See you later then."

The chief headed through the swinging doors and Donny turned back to me. "Nice seeing you again, Judge. Thanks for showing me how to get here."

"You Never Can Tell?" asked Dwight. "How old's that one?"

"1951," I said. "I've been wanting to see it for ages and Vallery Feldman at Blockbuster finally got it in for me. Dick Powell and Peggy Dow. She was in *Harvey.* Wonder what ever happened to her?"

"This isn't one of those goopy musicals, is it?"

"Trust me. Dick Powell's a dog who comes back to earth to find out who murdered him. There's a horse angel, too. You'll love it."

Dwight's not quite the old-movie addict I am unless it's set against the Second World War. Then we both cry when Van Heflin dies or John Payne throws himself on a hand grenade to save his comrades. (At least, *I* cry. Dwight always claims a summer cold or sinuses.)

Uncle Ash and Aunt Zell had already gone up to their room and I was in the kitchen waiting for Dwight to come before microwaving some popcorn.

The rain had begun again and I held the side screen open for him. His sandy brown hair was damp and his cowlick was standing straight up as he swiped at it.

"So how'd it go with Donny Turner?" I asked.

Dwight looked at his watch. "Fourteen seconds," he said. "Ed Gardner owes me five bucks."

"Excuse me?"

"I bet him I wouldn't be here two minutes before you asked about Turner. He thought you'd be more subtle and take at least five."

"Very funny. Just for that, we eat our popcorn plain tonight. No butter. No salt."

"Hey!"

I pinched him on the side just where a slight bulge was forming when he belted his jeans too tightly, and he quit grousing.

"Did y'all arrest him?" I persisted.

"We're a long way from another arrest. Of course, a lot of arsonists do start out fighting legitimate fires, then move on to setting them and he sure fits the profile."

"But?"

"No 'but.' We didn't push him hard. Just told him we wanted to get an idea of how long it takes people to respond to a fire call. What was he doing when he was paged? That sort of thing. Because Ed and his people haven't found any signs of a timing device. The pour patterns indicated that whoever did it seems to have sloshed gasoline around and lit a match right then, so we need to know where people were right before the alarms went off."

"Where was Donny?"

"Around. Coming home from a Little League ball game when the first fire started, home early and watching television with his parents when Mount Olive went up. Or so he says. We'll see."

"I take it that means you confirmed A.K.'s story?"

"Off the record?"

"Always." I held up my hand in the Boy Scouts' three-finger pledge of honor.

"Okay. Ed did reach out and touch the Pritchett woman today and she corroborated. ATF's still not ready to cut them loose though."

The lid was about to bounce off the popper bowl. I opened the microwave, poured some of the popped kernels into a big wooden bowl and put the rest back in to finish. Dwight snitched a few as we waited.

"Donny Turner tell you about how Charles Starling spray-painted their school bus once?"

"And how careless he is with cigarettes? Oh, yes indeed. Why do you think we're taking a closer look at Turner?"

"On the other hand," I said, "maybe it's not as obvious as it looks. What do you want to drink? Bourbon?"

"Beer if you've got it."

I pointed him toward the refrigerator.

"And what do you mean, not what it looks?" Dwight popped the top of a long-necked bottle and took a deep swallow. "If it's not racism or pyromania, what else would it be?"

"Murder?"

"Arthur Hunt? Who'd want to kill a harmless old drunk like Arthur Hunt?"

"I don't know. You're the detective. But the man *is*

dead and nobody seems to be paying much attention to that."

"We've paid attention," Dwight protested. "There's nothing there. No next-of-kin. No insurance on his life. Nobody threatened by him."

"I heard him threaten Reverend Ligon."

"When?"

"Sunday before last. Mr. Ligon fired him for drunkenness and Hunt said he was going to tell the deacons all about Ligon."

"Ligon sound worried?"

In all honesty, I had to say no. "But look at the results. Ligon wanted to enlarge the church and he couldn't get the votes to do it legitimately. Now with the fellowship hall out of the way and the most fortuitous end of the church burned, he can call in the architects and insurance money will foot most of the bill. Not to mention all the money that's been donated."

"Reverend Ligon?"

I had to admit it was hard to picture that very proper man with a gas can in one hand and spray paint in the other.

"He's not the only one who wanted to remodel," I said. "Maidie tells me there's a sizeable contingent that's burning to build."

Dwight grinned and I had to smile, too, as I realized what I'd said.

"All the same," he reminded me, "how many of them would know to use that brand of spray paint?"

I nodded. "Or know Starling's way of printing?"

The bell rang on the microwave and I dumped the rest of our popcorn into the big wooden bowl.

"A horse angel, huh?" said Dwight as we headed upstairs to my VCR.

❧ 24 ❧

God has planted us a garden
Man must keep it weeded.
   —Atherton Memorial Presbyterian

I didn't know if Cyl DeGraffenried was avoiding me since Monday evening or whether Doug had legitimately assigned her elsewhere, but Tracy Johnson prosecuted on Tuesday and Wednesday and she was there again on Thursday.

Tracy's tall and willowy with short blonde hair and gorgeous green eyes that she downplays in court with oversized, scholarly-looking glasses. Even though she loves high heels as much as I do, she's savvy enough to wear flats when arguing before vertically challenged male judges.

Thursday is usually catch-up day, but I'd worked hard to keep things moving the first three days and there wasn't all that much to catch up on.

"Be nice if we could finish early enough for me to get my hair done this afternoon," said Tracy during our morning break. "I'm driving down to the beach tomorrow afternoon."

"Suits me," I said. "Forty-five minutes for lunch?"

"I could be back in thirty."

We disposed of the last case at three-seventeen.

By four o'clock, I was on my way out of Dobbs, heading for the farm. The sun was finally shining again and after three days of rain, the air felt so hot and steamy I wanted to wring it out like a washcloth and hang it on a line somewhere to dry.

Passing Bethel Baptist, I almost ran off the road trying to see if I'd read their sign right:

> *Let the main thing*
> *Of the main thing*
> *Be the main thing*

Now what the hell did that mean?

I was almost tempted to stop at the parsonage and see if Barry Blackman could explain it to me. (Barry's the first boy I ever kissed and sometimes I have trouble taking him seriously as a preacher.)

As I turned off Forty-eight, I had to slow for a tractor pulling a long line of empty tobacco drags, getting ready for the start of barning season. When the way was clear, the child who was at the wheel waved me around and I gave her a wave back even though I didn't recognize her.

I was driving tractors back and forth between fields and barns when I was eleven and too little to do much

else to help get the crop in. I remember the first time I
was allowed to take an empty drag back to the field
without one of my brothers along—a touch of nervousness about rounding corners too fast or having to pull
the drag into a tight space, but also a vaulting pride at
being trusted with that much horsepower. By the end of
the summer, I was slinging nasties with the empty
trucks and maneuvering the full ones right up to the
bench.

Never turned over but one the whole summer, either.

I passed the King homeplace without seeing Mrs.
Avery, but down at the ashes of Burning Heart of God,
three black men were tossing debris into the back of a
large truck. The site was already looking neater, and if I
knew Mrs. Avery, that whole slope would be blooming in
azaleas come next spring.

At my house, I was thrilled by how much had been done
since Saturday. All the Sheetrock was up and the men
were trimming out the doors and windows. The kitchen
cabinets had been delivered and a plumber was in-
stalling my new washer. He'd already hooked up the
bathroom fixtures and the sound of flushing was loud in
the land when Will demonstrated. I couldn't say enough
in praise.

"You still want everything painted white?" my brother
asked.

"Everything except my bedroom," I said.

That was going to be a dark hunter green. With white
organdy curtains and shades, it would feel like a cool

woodsy glade in the summer. Heavier, darker drapes would make it cozy in winter.

Since the only major pieces of furniture I actually own outright are a chest that came from my mother's mother and a headboard that I'd bought when I was over at the High Point Furniture Market in the spring, I planned to start with a solid white interior and see what stood up and saluted once I acquired more furniture.

"April says she's got a desk and a sleeper couch if you want to come by and take a look."

I told him I'd run over there for a few minutes and be back before he left.

"Not unless you get back by five-thirty," he said. "Oh, and here. From now on, you'll need these."

He pulled a set of keys from his pocket and for the first time, it registered on me that the outer doors now had knobs and locks.

An official house.

And *me* the chatelaine.

It looked as if everyone had gone when I got over to Andrew's house. April's car and both trucks, too, were missing from yard and carport. I banged on the back door, stuck my head in and called, "Anybody home?"

"In here, Deborah."

I followed the sound of April's voice back to the den, where I found her sorting through boxes of papers. Her curly brown hair was cut short for the summer, and summer freckles sprinkled her face and arms and legs.

Her white shorts and blue shirt were both dirty, but her

face glowed as she gestured proudly to the wall behind her. "What do you think?"

"Hey, it really came out nice, didn't it?" I complimented.

April's as bad as Julia Lee. If she didn't love teaching so much, she could make a living at interior design and she is personally handy with a circular saw and hammer.

This house, for instance, began life as a 1920s bungalow that her uncle owned over in Makely. When he died, his son sold the lot to a supermarket and told April that she and Andrew could have the house as a wedding present if they'd move it. Since then, they've raised the roof to add a second floor and she keeps shifting walls the way other women rearrange furniture. Will doesn't think she really appreciates the significance of load-bearing walls and swears that one of these days, she's going to move one door hinge too many and the whole place is going to cave in. She just laughs and hands him a screwdriver.

Her latest project was making herself a real work space in the den. Before, she'd used a wooden desk, a metal file cabinet and some old mismatched bookcases. Now the space was filled with a sleek built-in unit that stretched from floor to ceiling and covered the whole wall. Below were file drawers and cabinets, above were bookshelves. There was a workstation on the countertop for the family's computer and printer and more counter space where she could spread out to grade papers.

"I want it," I said.

She laughed. "Can't have it. What you *can* have is my old desk."

The old desk was imitation mahogany and had looked okay before. Standing out in the middle of the room against the new backdrop though, it was pretty shabby.

"Give it a coat of red enamel or decoupage it and it'll look fine for now," said April.

She was right, of course, and besides, beggars can't be choosers. I pulled out one of the drawers. It seemed to be stuffed with sixth-grade spelling papers. "Do all teachers save this much paper? You're worse than Mrs. Avery."

"Is she a paper saver, too?"

"You better believe it! When I was over there the other day, she pulled out a note that I'd tried to pass to Portland when we were in her sophomore English class."

April gave a rueful laugh. "I would cluck in superior horror if I hadn't just found an absentee excuse from the mother of a student who graduated from college last month. I keep thinking I'm going to sort through and keep selected samples—you do like to see how the children compare from one year to another—but look at all these cartons! I'm tempted to just close my eyes and have A.K. take them all to the firehouse."

"Firehouse?"

"They have a recycling bin there for white paper. The dump recycles newspapers, magazines and corrugated cardboard but they're not into copier paper yet."

For a minute I hesitated, almost feeling a connection somewhere.

Then it was gone.

"How's it been going?" I asked. "With A.K. and everything?"

"Okay." Her bright face dimmed a little. Then she shrugged. "It kills me that he's going to have a record, but I keep reminding myself that it's not as if I had serious hopes of his going to Harvard or becoming a brain surgeon. All he's ever wanted to do is farm just like his daddy and a jail record certainly didn't hurt Andrew's ability to farm. So all in all . . ."

"A.K.'s a good kid," I said.

She smiled. "Oh, Deborah, honey, I do know that. But he doesn't always think. These three weekends may truly be what he's needed. A taste of what can happen if he's not more careful. He's going to be just fine."

"Okay," I said briskly. "Will said something about a sleeper couch?"

"Right. You may not have seen it before because we've had it up in the spare bedroom. Ruth's decided she wants to switch rooms, so we're going to get rid of it. It's one my Aunt Mildred had. The fabric's awful but it has good lines and the mattress is very comfortable."

I winced when I saw the blue and purple stripes with little pink morning glories twining in and out.

"We can reupholster it," she said brightly.

"Aunt Zell probably knows somebody."

"So do I, but it's a lot cheaper if we do it ourselves. Anyhow, let me know when you're ready for these things and I'll have them sent over."

I hugged her hard. "Thanks, neighbor."

* * *

Will was gone when I got back and I used my new keys to get inside and walk through the empty rooms. I noted how the late afternoon sunlight fell through the windows, looked at the view from the sunroom, saw from my screened porch how the pond reflected the willows and overhead clouds.

Nothing is certain in life and heaven knows the county is changing out from under our feet, but I thought how I might very well live out my life here. Fifty years from now I could be an arthritic old woman who sits on this very same porch to enjoy afternoon sunlight and to watch summer clouds float across a mirror-flat sheet of water.

Enter into thy kingdom and take possession.

I will plant pecan trees, I promised myself. I will have daylilies and gardenias, azaleas and irises, and all the flowers of my mother's garden. I will take cuttings of Aunt Zell's lilacs and Miss Sallie Anderson's pink roses and Daddy's figs. I'll dig dogwoods out of the woods and maples and willow oaks.

Deep inside my head, the preacher and the pragmatist nudged each other in the ribs and began to laugh. I ignored them. I would *too* make the time.

And yes, Haywood was going to have to move that damn greenhouse or I'd move it for him. It was just like—

"Ah," said the pragmatist, halting in mid-laughter. "Do you suppose—?"

The preacher sat very still, and then he nodded.

Parallel construction, I thought, remembering Mrs. Avery's English classes. Or did I mean math? If A is to B as C is to D, then A equals C?

More like C squared, I decided, as everything I'd observed over the last few weeks began to line up and make sense.

Carry a grudge and it gets heavier with every step.
　—Freedom Baptist Church

My phone line hadn't yet been connected, but even though I had my cell phone on the car, I didn't have a directory. I suppose I could have called 911 and explained that it wasn't really an emergency and could I please have the fire chief's home number, but in the end, it was easier to call Seth and ask him.

It took three calls to locate him, then two more to locate the deputy chief, who said No, not as far as he knew, but he could ask some of the others.

Dwight wasn't as obliging. He was off duty, he said. He had some fresh tomatoes from his mother's garden and was about to make himself a killer BLT as soon as the bacon thawed enough to prise off a few slices and no, running halfway across the county on a spur-of-the-moment whim wasn't how he'd planned to spend his evening, thank you very much.

I waited him out, then told him that if he didn't want

to come, I'd call Ed Gardner. Let Ed get all the glory.
Let the *Ledger* and the *News and Observer* make what
they would of the fact that Colleton County couldn't
take care of its own problems but had to have the Feds
solve it for them while its chief of detectives stayed
home to fix himself a tomato sandwich.

"Okay, *okay!* I'm on my way. Meet you at the firehouse in twenty-five minutes."

"Don't forget to get a search warrant from the magistrate," I said.

"Tell me again what we're looking for and where you
think we'll find it?"

"Well, I'm not completely sure," I admitted, "but you
should recognize it when you see it, and as for *where*—"
I quickly listed some general areas.

It was actually closer to thirty-five minutes before
Dwight rolled up at the firehouse. Unless he's expedit-
ing—blue lights flashing, siren howling—Dwight's one
of the slowest drivers I know.

While I waited, the volunteer on duty, a recent trans-
plant from Rochester, gave me the fifty-cent tour and I
was shamed into writing a check for their fund toward a
new fire truck. I looked at the large recycling bin for
collecting white office paper and no, he told me, he'd
never seen anybody rummaging through it, but that
wasn't to say they *couldn't.*

I casually dropped Donny Turner's name into the
conversation and that got me a glowing account of
young Turner's tireless dedication. "Donny checks by

here almost every night, even when he's not on call. He's up for Volunteer of the Year again this year."

We still had two good hours of daylight left when Dwight finally pulled in beside my car. He was followed by a patrol car with officers Jack Jamison and Mayleen Richards.

"I figure if I'm gonna search, I might as well have some help."

We drove in tandem out to the King homeplace.

Grace King Avery was watering her collection of flowering baskets on the screened back porch when our three cars came to a stop on her newly graveled driveway. She wore her usual cotton shirtdress—this one was pink— and her gray hair was tied back in a black ribbon. It was the first time I'd ever seen her without a bun. Retirement must be making her lax, I thought.

The white dog came to the screen door, nudged it open with his head and stood on the doorstep barking loudly.

"Smudge! Stop that this minute," she scolded.

Dogs are amenable. He stopped barking and began wagging his tail instead.

"Come in, come in," Mrs. Avery said, holding open the screen door and looking askance at the two uniformed officers behind me. "Is something wrong, Deborah?"

I murmured inconsequentially and introduced Jamison and Richards. Dwight she had met before.

"Oh, but where are my manners? Please! Do have a seat."

The house stood in a grove of ancient oak trees, some of them eight or ten feet in circumference and more than seventy feet tall. Despite the heat, the open porch was cool and shady. We had our choice of porch swing, rocking chairs or Adirondack chairs, all freshly painted in that notorious green enamel.

Since it was my idea, Dwight thought I should be the one to speak, so when she asked if this was an official visit, I said, "I'm afraid so. You see, Mrs. Avery, when Mount Olive's sexton died in that fire, the arson stopped being a simple felony and became a capital offense."

"Capital?" She sank down in the rocker next to mine and looked at me, appalled. Smudge pricked up his ears and came to stand by her chair as if to comfort her. "You mean that Raymond could be put to death?"

"If he and Starling were found guilty, yes."

"But surely they didn't intend for anyone to die. I'm *positive* they didn't know that poor man was there."

"Intent doesn't matter, ma'am," Dwight said. "Anybody who sets fire to a dwelling—"

Mrs. Avery was shaking her head. "It was a church!"

"It was also Arthur Hunt's dwelling," I said gently, suddenly feeling like a Judas. "He lived in that room at the back."

"So even if they didn't know it was a dwelling, they're still liable," Dwight said inexorably.

"But all the evidence isn't in place," I told her, "and

that's why we've come. Raymond Bagwell has been working for you how long?"

"I didn't move back here until I retired in May, but I'd hired Raymond, let me think . . . in March, it was. Yes, because I had him paint my bedroom before I came. And he's been working on the grounds. I wish you could remember what the flower gardens were like when my mother was alive. It's slow work bringing them back to life, but Raymond's been such a good hard worker."

She turned abruptly to Dwight. "Are you absolutely sure he's really involved? Maybe it was just the Starling boy alone. Isn't there some way to tell who did the spray-painting? Compare their handwriting or something?"

"They were together both nights," Dwight said. "They alibi each other."

"Oh." She took a deep breath and sank back in her chair in resignation. "You asked how long he's worked for me? Almost five months. And occasional jobs for my brother before that, of course. My brother died last November, you remember, and that's when the house and land passed to me."

"And Raymond had access to every part of it?"

"Access?" She seemed bewildered by my question.

"Maybe I should rephrase that," I said. "Were there any parts of the house or farm that you'd put off-limits to him? Any of the barns or shelters?"

"No, of course not. He had to be able to get to the

tools and equipment—the lawn mower, tractor, the rakes and shovels."

"What about the house? Basement, attic?"

"There is no basement. As for the attic, there's nothing up there for him. In fact, he never goes beyond the kitchen unless I need him to move a heavy piece of furniture."

"So the kitchen is the only place he would feel free to enter?"

Her neat gray head gave a firm nod. "And then only if I were here."

"There might be times though when you were gone and he was working outside alone?" I persisted.

"Well, yes, but—"

"Mrs. Avery, Major Bryant here has a warrant to search your house."

Dwight drew the warrant from the inner breast pocket of his sports jacket. Smudge cocked his head, but Mrs. Avery did not reach for it.

"Search? *My* house?"

"Yes, ma'am."

"Whatever for? I told you that he wasn't allowed— oh! You think he came in when I wasn't here?"

"Have we your permission?" I asked.

"Well, yes, of course, although if you brought a search warrant, it seems to me you don't need my permission, do you?"

She started to rise, but Dwight touched her arm and said, "Why don't you wait out here with Deborah, ma'am? It might be less upsetting for you."

As Dwight followed his two deputies inside, Mrs. Avery shook her head. "It's wicked, it is. Just wicked."

"The search?" I asked.

"That Raymond could be put to death for something he didn't even know he was doing."

Her distress seemed genuine as she pleated the soft cotton fabric of her skirt between her fingers. The dog put his head on her knee and she stroked his silky ears until some of the tension went out of her face.

We sat without speaking for a time and gazed out over the shady green lawns that stretched through new flower beds down to the branch. Beyond the dip of the branch, there wasn't much left of Burning Heart of God. Those workers had been industrious and had hauled away the burned-out trailer that had served as Sister Williams's home.

"I understand there was a reversion clause in the deed your grandfather gave the church."

"Such a surprise. But so fortuitous that I can hold it in trust for them," Mrs. Avery said with a touch of her usual complacency. "My grandfather was a farsighted man."

"Once you get rid of those old wrecked cars out by the little graveyard, this will be a pretty view."

"It was my grandmother's favorite place to sit when I was a little girl. Preacher Renfrow used to keep that little church pretty as a postcard. He and the congregation would get out twice a year and have cleanup day and you could hear them singing of a Sunday evening. So restful." She sighed.

"Things were different when Sister Williams took over," I said softly.

"Oh, Deborah, you don't know! I was just glad that Gramma wasn't here to see how trashy it got. I nearly *died* when she hauled that old trailer in. And now look over there at that garbage heap—smashed-up cars, old washing machine and refrigerator! Not that my brother ever noticed. 'Live and let live,' he'd say. 'It could be worse. We could have a shot house there or a house of bad women.' He didn't care *how* bad it looked. When he wasn't out on the tractor, he was inside watching television. He just didn't care."

"But you did."

"Well, of *course* I—" She broke off and her vehemence turned contemplative. "It was awful to see it burned like that, but in a way you can't really blame Raymond. I mean, here he was, working on this side to make everything beautiful again, while over there . . . I mean, it's not as if Sister Williams had a churchful of members."

"Didn't hurt much to burn Balm of Gilead either," I said.

"Exactly! They were going to tear it down anyhow. And Mount Olive's going to be finer than ever." Her voice faltered. "Only, that poor man. But to be passed out drunk at church—and on Sunday, too?"

"Good riddance to bad rubbish?" I asked bluntly.

"Oh, now, Deborah, it's not for us to judge the worth of a person."

The screen door opened and Dwight said, "Mrs.

Avery, we wonder if you could tell us about something in here?"

As she rose, Dwight caught my eye and gave an imperceptible nod.

We passed through the kitchen and, to my surprise, skirted the study where several cartons of school papers still waited for Mrs. Avery to sort through them.

"I see you still haven't thrown any of those papers away or sent them to be recycled," I said.

"Not yet. I've been too busy."

Dwight continued on upstairs and we trailed along. Smudge, too.

"Raymond came up here?" she asked. "What was he doing?"

At the end of the upper hall was a narrow, inconspicuous door that led to a steeper set of steps.

Mrs. Avery stopped short when she saw the open door. "The attic? What on earth—?"

Slowly she followed Dwight up the steps. The dog's nails clicked on the uncarpeted wood. Mrs. Avery was almost breathless when we came out under a roof with such a high pitch that even Dwight could stand up without worrying about banging his head. Jamison and Richards were there, too, and they wore white latex gloves to keep from contaminating the evidence.

Naked lightbulbs hung down from the rafters. It was hot up here, but ventilator fans in the roof kept it from being unbearable. For such an old house, the attic was surprisingly uncluttered. Boxes and trunks lined the sides, but the middle space was completely empty except for several pieces of thin plywood lying face down along the tops of the boxes, which were piled chest-high. The largest piece of plywood was no more than eight feet long by twelve or fourteen inches wide, the smallest measured something like four feet by eight inches. There must have been half a dozen pieces.

Slowly, the deputies turned them on edge so that we could see what was lettered there in green paint—the same racist epithets repeated over and over in nearly identical letters. A spray can stood on the floor next to a pair of paint-speckled yellow rubber gloves.

Mrs. Avery put out her hand to steady herself on the stair railing. "I don't understand. Why would Raymond—"

"No, Mrs. Avery. Not Raymond. You." Dwight held out a sheet of ruled notebook paper covered with lines written in pencil. At the top of the sheet was the student's name: *Charles Starling, English II.* The paper was covered with a fine green mist and certain words were underlined in red pencil. *Bigger,* for instance, had been written with the same combination of capitals and small letters as the *nigger* on the boards.

I had hoped they would discover samples of Starling's school papers in a compromising hiding place. Finding her actual practice boards was gravy on the tree, as Haywood is fond of saying.

"You were in court the day the boys were tried for vandalism," I said, "and you realized that they had just given you a perfect way to get rid of that eyesore across the branch. You would burn down some black churches, sandwiching raggedy little Burning Heart of God in the middle, and pray Starling got all the blame because it would be only his printing on the walls."

"That's ridiculous!" she snapped. "Really, Deborah."

"Not half as ridiculous as you pretending you didn't know your grandfather had placed a restriction on that church deed. As carefully as you've researched your family's records for the past four hundred years? I don't think so. If we look through your scrapbooks, I bet we'll find copies of every deed your family's ever held."

"You leave my scrapbooks alone!" she said sharply. "I won't have you touching them!"

Officer Mayleen Richards rolled her eyes as she sealed the spray can and the gloves in separate plastic bags. Dwight was doing the same with the notebook paper.

"Fingerprints," I said succinctly and Mrs. Avery flinched as the full implications began to sink in.

"No! It was Raymond. Raymond and Charles."

"A man died because you couldn't stand an eyesore on land that used to belong to your grandfather."

"No one was supposed to get hurt," Mrs. Avery said, the beginning of a whimper in her voice. "It was his own fault. Really it was. If he hadn't been drinking, he could have walked away in plenty of time."

She held out her hand to Dwight beseechingly. "Surely you can understand that? It wasn't my fault."

❦ 26 ❦

Faith is a way of walking, not talking.
—Pisgah Church

Isaac Mitchiner was buried beside his sister, Cyl's mother, in the cemetery at Mount Olive, a hundred feet away from where he had lain for twenty-one years. The graveside service, simple and direct, was conducted by Reverend Ligon with the assistance of Reverend Freeman.

The hot morning sun poured down on us. The choir sang "Safe in the Arms of Jesus" and "There Is a Rock That Is Higher."

I went.

Wallace Adderly didn't.

Cyl sat amongst her light-skinned family and I remembered her saying that when her cousins jeered, Isaac had comforted her—"We're the only true Africans."

As I passed through the line afterwards, she clasped my hand with a wry smile. "I still owe you dinner."

"Yes, you do."

"Thank you for coming," she said.

"You're welcome," I said.

Daddy called me near the end of July. He doesn't like to talk on the telephone, so his conversations are always short and to the point.

"You gonna be out this way tomorrow evening?"

"Didn't plan to, but I can if you want me to. Why?"

"Thought you might like to see that there angel go back up."

"What time?"

" 'Bout six?"

"No problem."

"Fine. See you then, shug."

He was waiting for me beside his old beat-up Chevy truck and I stood on tiptoe to kiss his leathery cheek. It was as hot and dusty as the first evening we'd driven out to the Crocker family cemetery.

The cotton was waist-high now and full of big white blooms and tiny little green bolls.

Once again, Rudy Peacock's big two-ton truck was there beside the low stone wall that enclosed the small graveyard, only this time, a bulky form stood in the bed of the truck. It was wrapped in burlap sacks and secured with strong, light cables.

A.K.'s black pickup was there, too. He and Raymond Bagwell had spent the last two hours raking and tidying away all the final bits and pieces of broken granite. The graveyard was as neat as Aunt Zell's living room.

No sign of Charles Starling. Probably too *Little House on the Prairie* for him.

Somehow, I wasn't surprised to see Smudge come running through the cotton rows.

Raymond shrugged. "Mrs. Avery's daughter's going to take him back to Washington with her after school starts. I told her I'd take care of him till then."

Gambling that her age and previously unblemished record would get her a quick parole, Mrs. Avery had accepted the plea bargain she'd been offered and was already serving time down in Atlanta. She might could have mounted a defense of insanity. Certainly her obsession with restoring the King family homeplace held a touch of madness. Instead, rather than defend her person, she'd opted to spend her money defending the land and, to her daughter's dismay, had retained Zack Young to fight Sister Williams's lawsuit to reclaim that newly landscaped acre.

Rudy Peacock was even bigger and more muscular than I'd remembered. Shyer, too.

"Did the wing take drilling?" I asked. "Or did you have to carve a whole new set?"

"Your nephew here got lucky," he said, not quite meeting my gaze. "Everything worked perfect. Would you believe I found a piece of granite the same exact shade in my scrap pile? It'd been out there so long, it even weathered good. 'Course, y'all will have to tell me if you think I'm as good a carver as my dad was."

As he spoke, he troweled fresh mortar onto the angel's pedestal.

"Now when I lower her down," he told A.K. and Raymond, "y'all got to make sure she's on here straight and hold her down, okay?"

"Okay," they chorused.

Peacock pulled himself up into the bed of the truck and attached the hook on his hydraulic winch to the cable wrapped around the angel. Then he pushed some buttons and the arm of the winch slowly rose in the air. When the angel was clear of the bed, he pushed another button and the arm ponderously swung the angel out over the wall.

"Little more this way," A.K. called. "Little more . . . little more . . . stop!"

He and Raymond grabbed the statue and steadied it straight over the pedestal. "Down a little . . . more . . . perfect!"

The angel settled gently onto her former perch and while the boys continued to hold her steady, Rudy Peacock removed the cable and burlap.

He used a small edging trowel to clean up the excess mortar, then stepped back proudly. "What do you think?"

"Beautiful!" we told him.

She was as naively sculpted as when I first saw her and her features still showed the effects of weathering, but the new wing tip was almost indiscernible and he had buffed her all over so that she gleamed in the late afternoon sunlight. No one would ever mistake this angel for a Renaissance creation, but here in this cotton field, open to all the elements, she would serve the Crockers another generation or two.

Daddy brought out his checkbook. "How much I owe you, Rudy?"

"Your money's no good with me, Mr. Kezzie," he said. "These two here already give me something on it and they're going to work off the rest. My youngest boy's going off to college next month and he don't want to do this anymore. Says it's too near like work, so I been needing more help."

"Well, I sure do appreciate it," Daddy said. "Looks real good."

A.K. and Raymond swarmed up over the truck, secured the winch hook and the cables, and folded up the burlap sacking.

With a wave of his hand, Rudy Peacock headed back down the lane, kicking up a cloud of white dust as he went.

The boys put their rakes and baskets in the back of A.K.'s pickup. Raymond whistled for the dog, who came running and jumped up on the tailgate, then A.K. slammed it shut and the two boys climbed in front.

Daddy continued to lean against the fender of his truck with a cigarette in his hand and I was sitting cross-legged atop the stone wall.

"Ain't—*aren't* y'all coming?" A.K. asked.

"We'll be along directly," said Daddy, who has never handed out praise too freely. "Boy?"

"Yessir?"

"I'm right pleased with you."

Blue eyes met blue eyes. A.K. nodded, settled his ball cap more firmly on his head and turned the key in his ignition.

Soon, even the sound of his truck faded in the distance and Daddy and I were alone together.

A new moon hung in the western sky, so new it was no more than the thinnest sliver of silver against the deepening blue. A bright planet—Jupiter? Venus?—gleamed nearby and I sent a mental kiss to Kidd, who would be coming this weekend to help me move into my new house.

Daddy finished his cigarette and came to join me on the wall.

We sat in easy silence for a long while, then, almost as if he was talking to himself, Daddy said, "Uncle Yancy over yonder, he died 'fore I come along but they say he could outfiddle the devil. I was always sorry I never heared him. And ol' Ham here, he surely did like peach brandy. He'd bring me enough pitted peaches ever' summer to run him off a gallon or two."

"Who was Mallie Crocker?" I asked, pointing to a nearby stone.

"Mallie? She was a Wiggins 'fore she married Ham's brother. All them Wiggins girls had the prettiest yellow hair. Real thick and curly . . ."

His voice trailed off and I knew his mind was running back through the years to when the people beneath these stones had lived and loved and quarrelled and laughed.

I scooted closer and leaned my head on his shoulder.

"When I was a boy growing up, a lot of my friends was nervous around graveyards, didn't like to be in 'em after dark. Myself, I always thought they was real peaceful places. Still do."

"But not for a long time," I said. "Okay?"

"Not till you're a old, old woman," he promised—as he'd been promising from the first day I realized parents could actually die—and his calloused hand squeezed mine with as much comfort as we're allowed in this uncertain world.

LATE AUGUST

Afternoon shadows shaded the dip in the deserted dirt road where a battered Chevy pickup sat with the motor idling. On the driver's side, a puff of pale blue smoke drifted through the open window as the old man inside lit a cigarette and waited. The two dogs in back tasted the sultry air and one of them stuck its head through the sliding rear window. The man reached up and rubbed the silky ears.

A few minutes later, a green Ford pickup approached from the opposite direction and pulled even with the Chevy. The old man acknowledged them with a nod, then stubbed out his cigarette and dropped it on the sandy roadbed.

"Evening, Mr. Kezzie," said the stocky, heavyset

1

driver who appeared to be in his early fifties. His hair was thinning across the crown and his face was lined from squinting through a windshield at too many sunrises.

The other, younger man was probably early thirties. He wore a neat blue shirt that had wet sweat circles under the arms.

Kezzie Knott peered past the driver. "This your cousin's boy?"

The older man nodded. "Norwood Love, Ben Joe's youngest."

"I knowed your daddy when he was a boy," Kezzie said, tapping another cigarette from the crumpled pack in his shirt pocket. "Good man till they shipped him off to Vietnam."

"That's what I hear." Norwood Love's jaw tightened. "I only knowed him after he come back."

And won't asking for no pity, thought Kezzie as he took a deep drag on his cigarette. Well, that part won't none of his business. Exhaling smoke, he said, "He the one taught you how to make whiskey?"

"Him and Sherrill here."

"I done told him, Mr. Kezzie, how you won't have no truck with a man that makes bad whiskey," his cousin said earnestly. "Told him ain't nobody never gone blind drinking stuff you had aught to do with."

"And that's the way I aim to keep it," Kezzie said mildly as he examined the cigarette in his gnarled fingers. There was no threat in his voice, but the young man nodded as if taking an oath.

2

"All I use is hog feed, grain, sugar and good clean water. No lye or wood alcohol and I ain't never run none through no radiator neither."

Kezzie Knott heard the sturdy pride in his voice. "Ever been caught?"

"No, sir."

"Sherrill says you got a safe place to set up."

"Yessir. It's—"

Kezzie held up his hand. "Don't tell me. Sherrill's word's good enough. And your'n." His clear blue eyes met the younger man's. "Sherrill says you was thinking eight thousand?"

"I know that's a lot, but—"

"No, it ain't. Not if you're going to do a clean operation, stainless steel vats and cookers."

He leaned over and took a thick envelope from the glove compartment and passed it over to Norwood Love. "Count it."

When the younger man had finished counting, he looked up at the other two. "Don't you want me to sign a paper or something?"

"What for?" asked Kezzie Knott, with the first hint of a smile on his lips. "Sherrill's told you my terms and you aim to deal square, don't you?"

"Yessir."

"Well, then? Ain't no piece of paper gonna let me take you to court if you don't."

"I reckon not."

"Besides"—a sardonic tone slipped into his voice—"there don't need to be nothing connecting

3

me to you if your place ain't as safe as you think it is."

As Norwood Love started to thank him, Kezzie Knott touched the brim of his straw hat to them, then put the truck in gear and pulled away through August heat and August humidity that had laid a haze across the countryside.

Ought to've paid more mind to the noon weather report, the old man told himself as he headed the truck toward home. Thick and heavy as this air was, he reckoned they might get another thunderstorm before bedtime.

Automatically he took a mental inventory of the farm—not just the homeplace but all the land touching his that his sons now owned and farmed.

Cotton was holding up all right, and soybeans and corn could take a little more rain without hurting bad, but all this water was leaching nutrients from the sandy soil. Bolls was starting to crack though so it was too late to spray the cotton with urea to get the nitrogen up enough to finish it off. Tobacco had so much water lately, it was all greened up again. Curing schedule shot to hell. Just as well, he supposed, since the ground was so soggy along the bottoms you couldn't get tractors in without bogging down.

Playing hell with the garden, too. Maidie was fussing about watery tomatoes and how mold on the field peas was turning 'em to mush. That second sowing of butter beans won't be faring so good neither—them fuzzy yellow beetle larvy making lace

4

outen the leaves. Every time him or Cletus dusted 'em, along come the rain to wash off all the Sevin before it had a chance to kill 'em.

The boys was worried, but that's what it was to be a farmer. First you lay awake praying for rain, then you lay awake praying for it to quit. You done it 'most your whole life, he thought. All them years Sue tried to make you put farming over whiskey. Got to be a habit after a while. Certainly was for the boys.

And now another round of hurricanes setting up to blow in more rain?

Deb'rah won't going to be any happier 'bout more rain than the boys. She said she was about to get eat up out there by the pond. Fish couldn't keep up with the eggs them mosquitoes was laying in this weather.

Through the open back window, Ladybelle's nose nudged the back of his neck. Kezzie took a final drag on his cigarette and stubbed the butt in his overflowing ashtray.

"Still don't see why she had to go and build out there when the homeplace is setting almost empty," he grumbled to the dogs.

CHAPTER | 1

> The situation . . . is portrayed day by day exactly as it existed, and is not the product of imaginings of writers who put down what the conditions should have been; the storm has been followed from its inception.

August 31—Hurricane Edouard is now 31° North by 70.5° West. Wind speed approx. 90 knots. (Note: 1 kt. = 1 nautical mile per hour.) (Note: a nautical mile is about 800 ft. longer than a land mile or .15 of a land mi.)

Math was not Stan Freeman's strongest subject. In the margin of his notebook, the boy laboriously scribbled the computations so he'd have the formula handy:

90 kts. =

90 + (90 x .15) =

He rummaged in his bookbag for his calculator.

The fan in his open window stirred the air but did little to cool the small bedroom. Perspiration gleamed on his dark skin. His red Chicago Bulls tank top clung damply to his chest. It'd been an oversized Christmas present from his little sister Lashanda, yet was already too tight. His distinctly non-stylish sneakers lay under the nightstand so his feet could breathe free. Three sizes in six months. After he outgrew a new pair in one month, Kmart look-alikes were all his mother would buy "till your body settles down."

At eleven and a half, it was as if his limbs had suddenly erupted. The pudginess that had lingered since babyhood was gone now, completely melted away into bony arms and legs that stretched him almost as tall as his tall father. He was glad to be taller. Short kids got no respect. Now if he could just do something about his head. It felt out of proportion, too big for his gangling body, and he kept his bushy hair clipped as short as his mother would allow so as not to draw attention to the disparity.

At the moment, though, he wasn't thinking of his appearance. Using his light-powered calculator, he multiplied ninety by point fifteen, then finished writing out his conversion:

90 + (13.5) = 103.5 mph.

For a moment, Stan lay back on his bed and imagined himself standing in a hundred-and-four miles per hour wind.

Freaking cool!

And never going to happen this far inland, he reminded himself. He sat up again and picked up where he'd left off in his main notes: *Hurricane warnings posted from Cape Lookout to Delaware, but forecasters predict that Edouard will probably miss the North Carolina coast.*

Gloomily, he added, *Hurricane Fran downgraded to a tropical storm last night.*

With a sigh as heavy as the humid August air the fan was pulling through his open window, Stan took out a fresh sheet of notebook paper and made a new heading.

NOTES—Meterolg

He paused, consulted the dictionary on the shelf beside his bed, tore out the sheet of paper and began again.

NOTES—Meteorologists say we're getting more tropical storms this year because of a rainy summer in the deserts of W. Africa. (Reminder—look up name of desert) (Reminder—look up name of country) This makes tropical waves that can turn into storms. At least they think that's what caused Arthur and Bertha so early this year.

He couldn't help wishing for the umpteenth time that he'd known about this new school's sixth-grade science project earlier in the summer. If he had, he might have thought about documenting the life and death of a killer hurricane in time for it to do some good. Unfortunately, nobody'd mentioned the project till this past week, a full month after Bertha did her number on Wrightsville Beach. Cesar and Dolly had been right on her heels, but both of them wimped out without making landfall.

Like Hurricane Edouard was about to do.

Just his luck if the rest of hurricane season stayed peaceful. When he came up with the idea of doing a day-by-day diary of a killer storm, Edouard was still kicking butt in the Caribbean and had people down at the coast talking about having to evacuate by Labor Day. Now, though . . .

He wasn't wishing Wilmington any more bad luck, but a category 3 or 4 hurricane would sure make a bitchin' project.

Sorry, God, he thought, automatically casting his eyes heavenwards.

"Son, I know you think you have to say things like that to be cool with the other kids," Dad chided him recently. "But you let it become a habit and one of these days, you're going to slip and say it to your mother and how cool will you feel then?"

Not for the first time, Stan considered the parental paradox. His father might be the preacher, but it was his mother who had all the Thou Shalt Nots engraved on her heart.

As if she'd heard him think of her, Clara Freeman tapped on the door and opened it without waiting for his response.

"Stanley? Didn't you hear me calling you?"

9

"Sorry, Mama, I was working on my science project."

Clara Freeman's face softened a bit at that. Guiltily, Stan knew that schoolwork could always justify a certain amount of leeway.

Yet schoolwork seldom took precedence over church work.

"Leave that for later, son. Right now, what with all the rain we've been having, Sister Jordan's grass needs cutting real bad and I told her you'd be glad to go over this morning and do it for her."

Without argument, Stan closed the notebook and placed it neatly on his bookshelf, then began cramming his feet into those gawdawful sneakers. His face was expressionless but every cussword he'd ever heard surged through his head. Bad enough that this wet and steamy August kept him cutting their own grass every week without Mama looking over the fences to their neighbors' yards. Sister Jordan had two teenage grandsons who lived right outside Cotton Grove, less than a mile away, but Mama could be as implacable as the Borg—which he'd only seen on friends' TV since Mama didn't believe in it for them. If ever she saw an opportunity to build his character through Christian sacrifice, resistance was futile.

Any argument and she'd be on her knees, begging God's forgiveness for raising such a lazy, self-centered son, begging in a soft sorrowful voice that always cut him deeper than any switch she might have used.

On the other hand, if he spent the next hour cutting Sister Jordan's grass, Mama wouldn't fuss about him going over to Dobbs with Dad this evening.

This was the second time they'd made love. The first had been in guilty haste, an act as irrational as gulping too much sweet cool water after days of wandering in a dry and barren land.

And just as involuntary.

Today they lay together on the smooth cotton sheets of her bed, away from any eyes that might see or tongues that might tell. Despite the utter privacy, and even though her mouth and body had responded just as passionately, just as hungrily as his, her lovemaking was again curiously silent. No noisy panting, no long ecstatic sobs, no outcries.

Cyl moaned only once as her body arched beneath his, a low sound that was almost a sigh, then she relaxed against the cool white sheets and murmured, "Holy, holy, holy."

"Don't," Ralph Freeman groaned. "Please don't."

She turned her face to his, her brown eyes bewildered. "Don't what?"

"Don't mock."

"*Mock*? Oh, my love, I would never mock you."

"Not me," he said miserably. "God."

She traced the line of his cheek with her fingertips. "I wasn't mocking," she whispered. "I was thanking Him."

11

* * *

Over in Dobbs, Dr. Jeremy Potts decided he'd put it off as long as he could. Having slept in this morning, he'd had to wait till late afternoon to go running. This hot and humid August had kept his resentments simmering. If not for the three biggest bitches of Colleton County, he told himself, he could be working out in the lavish air-conditioned exercise room at the country club instead of running laps on a school track under a broiling sun. He could follow that workout with a refreshing shower instead of driving back to his condo dripping in sweat. Thanks to his ex-wife who'd been wound up by her lawyer's wife, not to mention that judge who gave Felicia everything but the gold filling in his back molar, it would be at least another two years before he could afford the country club's initiation fees and monthly dues.

Thank you very much, Lynn Bullock, he thought angrily as he laced up his running shoes.

Jason Bullock hefted his athletic bag over his shoulder and paused in the doorway to watch his wife brush her long blonde hair. She had a trick of bending over and brushing it upside down so that it almost touched the floor, then she'd sit up and flip her head back so that her hair fell around her pretty heart-shaped face with a natural fluffiness.

"See you later, then, hon. I'll grab a hot dog at the field and be home around eight, eight-thirty."

"For the love of God, Jase! Don't I mean *any*thing to you?" Lynn asked impatiently, speaking to

12

his reflection in her mirror. She pushed her hair into the artfully tangled shape she wanted and set it in place with a cloud of perfumed hair spray. "I won't be here later, remember? Antiquing with my sister? Her and me spending the night in a motel up around Danville? I can't believe you—"

"Only kidding," he said. "You don't think I'd really forget that I'm a bachelor on the prowl tonight, do you?" With his free hand, he stroked a mock mustache and gave her a wicked leer.

"And don't try to call me because we're going to ramble till we get tired and then stop at the first motel we come to."

It pleased her when his leer was replaced by a proper expression of husbandly concern.

"You'll be careful, won't you, honey? Don't let Lurleen talk you into staying somewhere that's not safe just because it's cheap, okay?"

"Don't worry. It'll be safe. And I'll call you soon as I'm checked in."

In the mirror, Lynn watched her husband leave. Not for the first time she wondered why she bothered to try and keep this marriage going. Except that Jason was going to *be* somebody in this state someday and she was going to be right there by his side. No way was she planning to wind up like her mother (after three husbands and five affairs, she was living on social security in a trailer park in Wake County) or Lurleen (only one husband but God alone knew how many lovers, one of which had left her with herpes and she was just lucky it wasn't AIDS). Besides, she'd busted her buns working double shifts at the hospital while Jase got his law degree so they wouldn't have a bunch of debt hanging over them when he started practicing. Now that the long grind was finally over, now that they could start thinking about a fancier house, a winter cruise, maybe even a trip to Hawaii, she wasn't about to blow it.

But that doesn't mean I've got to keep putting my needs on hold, Lynn thought, absently caressing her smooth cheek. Jase used to be such a tiger in bed. This summer, between long hours at the firm and weekends at the ball field or volunteer fire department—"building contacts" was how he justified so much time away—all he wanted to do in bed most nights was sleep.

Not her.

She took a dainty black lace garter belt from her lingerie drawer and put it in her overnight case. Black hose and a push-up bra followed. She dug out a pair of strappy heels from the back of her closet and put those in, too. Panties? Why bother? You won't have them on long enough to matter, she told herself with a little shiver of anticipation.

She thought about calling Lurleen, but her sister was going to Norfolk this weekend and wouldn't be home to answer the phone anyhow if Jase should call. Not that he would. He wasn't imaginative enough to play the suspicious husband. And no point giving Lurleen another hold over her. She already knew too much.